Another Messiah

by Stuart Rawlings

Sierra Dreams Press

Published by Sierra Dreams Press
15200 Wild Oak Lane, Auburn, CA 95603
(530) 878-8831
www.sierradreamspress.com
stuartrawlings@hughes.net

First Edition 2005
Second Edition 2019
Also available in e-Book and Audiobook formats
ISBN-13: 978-0-9771405-4-1

Edited by Walter Kleine
Cover and chapter art by Phawnda Moore
www.journalismdesign.net
Back cover photograph by Jeff Hendriksen
www.filmworksphotography.com
Second Edition typeset by VivoCreative.Group

Contents

Preface

At 8:20 am on March 15, 2004, I was sitting in a café in Weed, California, thinking that this would be like most other days in my life. I was savoring every bite of the poached eggs, waffles and bacon, which are not part of the normal routine in my home in Auburn, California. In my booth were the two people whom I love most in this world—my Brazilian wife, Elsa, and our four-year-old son, Austin. I had just done some adoption work for a family whose home looked out at beautiful snow-covered Mount Shasta.

Who knows where special energy comes from in a long life? Perhaps it was from an orange sunrise peeping through the window, which moved our waitress to draw the blinds. Maybe it was the mystery of the nearby magic mountain. Or maybe it was the headline in the local newspaper which predicted the re-election of President George W. Bush. In any case, I borrowed a pen from the cashier, moved my waffle to the side, placed my white paper napkin in front of me, and started to write.

I did not think about the words. They just flowed, as if a life force within me needed me to escape to some more tangible form outside. Since writing during breakfast is not normal behavior, my wife said something like, "What are you doing?"

I gave her a vague response which included the word "novel."

The special energy stayed with me that day. When we reached home, I took out the napkin and transferred the scribbling to my computer. I looked at the writing, sort of liked it, and suspected that it would never amount to anything.

Four months later, while visiting my friend Frank

Satterthwaite in Rhode Island, we started talking about writing. He was working on a book about career objectives. I told him that I would be more interested in his first novel. I also revealed that I had one that was on the back, back burner. That night, we watched Senator John Kerry trot out his Vietnam Swift Boat comrades in an awkward attempt to persuade America that he would be strong in a time of war. "You know that novel I mentioned," I said to Frank. "If Kerry loses this election, I think I'll write it. It'll give me something to do—like therapy."

And so it happened. Kerry lost in November, and one day in early January of 2005, I went to my computer and double-clicked on a file called "Messiah." Again the life force drove words out of me, and my fingers could barely keep up. I had no control over the product. No notion of what might happen next. My body was just a conduit for an alien living inside me. My mind traveled back to some places where I had lived, and to others where I had never been. I moved freely between fiction and non-fiction. For the most part, my normal life continued—a full-time job with Placer County Mental Health, more work with Adopt International, teaching night courses at Chapman and National Universities, mediating a new law case, singing with a quartet called the Auburnaires, trying to spend as much time as possible with my wife and son—and then, at the very end of each day, squeezing in time on the novel.

On March 24, 2005, I finished it—thirty chapters and 45,000 words. For most of April I worked with friends on editing and proofreading. For most of May, I looked for an agent or publisher and found none. I also discovered that this route might take up to two years to publish, and I didn't want to wait that long. I decided to start my own publishing company—*Sierra Dreams Press*, and to have the novel published by October.

Each time I read this book, I have a special feeling toward it. It's not just a path for me to try to seek fame or fortune. It's not just an extension of my ego, or some kind of personal pursuit. It's not just entertainment—although all these are parts of it, too. Much more important, I believe this book has a message for mankind. If we continue our present behavior toward nature, toward others, and toward ourselves, our race will not have much of a future. This book offers an alarm, and a global view which may be useful in today's world.

—Stuart Rawlings
    Auburn, California
    October 15, 2005

CHAPTER ONE

Nativity

And it came to pass, at the start of the twenty-first century after the birth of Jesus, that much of the land was in chaos. Religious and patriotic zeal, weapons of mass destruction, environmental devastation, global warming, greed, hunger, poverty, and floods were just a few of the forces ruling over Planet Earth. And there were no clear answers or even approaches to these problems. There were no policies which seemed to be working, and no people to whom the conscientious ones on this planet might turn for help.

One day—it is not known precisely when or where—a child was born in a home in the Old City of Jerusalem. There was no bright star in the sky that night, no wise men or women who came bearing gifts, and no indication that this was anything but a normal birth—one of millions which took place every day on the planet.

The mother's name was Hagar, taken from the maidservant of Abraham who had given birth to Ishmael at the site now known as Mecca. The father was unknown. Hagar was only fourteen, and nothing was known about her background. At the time of the birth, those in attendance believed that Hagar may have been a prostitute, may have been raped, or maybe didn't even know what made babies. She may have been Jewish, Islamic, Christian, a combination of these, or none of them.

The delivery was long and hard, and the mother died soon after it was finished. The child was a girl. Her legs were withered, and although the attendants slapped her on the back and bottom to fill her with life, she did not utter a single sound. Several attendants, knowing the difficulty of raising such a child, suggested that it be put to death. No one would know, and the world might be better off. But one attendant, called Maya, said no—the baby should be spared, and that she would raise it.

For some reason, the child was never given a name. Perhaps the new mother was afraid that this would attract attention and lead to problems. Perhaps it was that the child had not yet developed into a being who could be described by a name. At any rate, the child was raised in Maya's home in Jerusalem—a tiny room in the back of a merchant's hut. She came to be known as just "the girl."

As the child grew, it became apparent that she would never have a normal body—never be able to walk or talk. She was never taken to a physician. Some people believed that she might be autistic, have multiple sclerosis, or be afflicted with a combination of such ailments. Some took one look at her and considered that she was lucky to be alive and to have anyone who might give her sustenance.

As time passed, there was a quality which some people noticed: her smile. It radiated a special warmth which reached inside of those around her and made them feel blessed. No one knew where this smile came from—indeed, it was said that this girl had nothing to smile about. But every so often, sometimes when least expected, there it was.

Little is known about the early life of the girl. She lived in a tiny bare room with her mother, whose main occupation appeared to be begging for food. Maya always dressed her in a white robe with a slight shade of pink. Maya was very protective of her daughter, and never left her alone. They rarely left the street on which they lived. They clung to each other, while watching the world around them. The girl ate, slept, performed basic bodily functions, was carried around by her mother, and never uttered a sound.

When the girl was three years old, a curious incident happened so fast that it was soon forgotten by those who were there. Three old men came to the door of the house and knocked. They were dressed in maroon robes and appeared to be kind, yet nervous. After the merchant invited them to come in, they asked to see the girl. They were led to Maya's room in the back, where the little girl lay on the floor. When she saw them, her eyes grew large and she immediately started to cry, with big tears running down her tiny cheeks. The old men also began to cry, weeping out loud, and they bowed down on the floor and prayed. The little girl reached out with her tiny hands and touched each of them in turn.

Some said later that these visitors were an entourage of rinpoches from Tibet, sent in search of an incarnated child after the death of a Buddhist leader, but there was no prominent Buddhist leader who had died recently. Nor was there any report of a cane or cup, or other sacred object, shown to the girl to evidence special qualities. And no one came later to bring her to Lhasa, Dharamsala, or any other place for traditional Tibetan Buddhist teaching. Nothing.

At the age of five, the little girl was sent five days a week to a non-sectarian school for the deaf in Old Town Jerusalem. She interacted some with other children her age, but also kept a distance from them. Her teacher tried to instruct her in sign language, but this failed. There was no lack of intelligence, for her eyes were intent on listening to everything that was said to her. She smiled when others laughed, again without uttering a sound. She was particularly interested when her teacher read the news of the day—about what was happening in Jerusalem, Israel, and other parts of the world. Having worked with deaf children for many years, the teacher believed that the little girl was holding back all communication and, that some day, at the right time, she would break her silence.

On her seventh birthday, the little girl was given a very special present by one of the Catholic nuns who visited her school. She received a motorized wheelchair. Since the girl had no movement in her legs, but some use of her arms and hands, she was thenceforth able to go places by herself. Upon receiving this gift, the girl looked at the nun with infinite gratitude, but there was also a slightly detectable look of strength—a quality few had ever noticed. At that moment, the nun smiled back and looked deeply into the child's eyes. And then, like the early visitors in maroon robes, the nun bowed down to the floor, wept, and prayed.

It did not take long for the child to learn how to direct her wheelchair. With help from Maya, she soon learned to navigate the cobblestone streets of the Old City. She learned how to avoid cars, donkeys, and people carrying merchandise. She learned how to visit the religious shrines—the Dome of the Rock, the Wailing Wall, and the Via Dolorosa—and to return safely home. She spent one whole day at Yad Vashem, the memorial to Jews who died in the holocaust. Later she went with Maya on longer trips by bus—to Bethlehem, to visit the birthplace of Jesus, to Masada, where Jews were massacred by Romans in 73 AD, and to towns such as Nablus and Ramalla in the "occupied" territories.

One morning, just a few months after her seventh birthday, gunshots were heard in the Jerusalem neighborhood of the little girl. There were shouts, the sound of running footsteps, and the rumbling of heavy vehicles. More shots were fired, and a man opened the door of the merchant's store to warn him that he and the other residents there must leave.

As they filed out, the merchant tried to lead them away from the noise and the danger—but the little girl did not follow him. She steered her wheelchair directly toward the noise—and her mother let her go, as if understanding that there was some higher purpose involved than personal safety. In a plaza, not far away, a column of Israeli tanks appeared. There were more shouts from several directions, and then the sound of automatic weapons.

As the little girl wheeled her chair into the center of the plaza, yelling was directed at her from both sides, telling her to go back.

She did not.

Instead, she moved to the exact center of the square and faced the tanks, which had stopped a short distance away. There were more shouts for her to leave, and she did not. The lead Israeli tank then pointed its immense gun barrel directly at the little girl.

Then there was silence, as both Israeli and Palestinian gunfighters stared at the scene and pondered what to do.

There are differing accounts of what happened next.

Some say an Israeli commander yelled that she was wired with explosives and should be blown up immediately. Others say that a Palestinian commander, noting the distraction of the girl, gave the order for his soldiers to fire at the Israeli forces. In any case, the following events were recorded:

The little girl spoke for the first time in her life, stating in clear Hebrew for all to hear, a single word, "*Maspeek!*" (Enough!)

Immediately afterward, the lead Israeli tank tried to fire its gun and blow her to the heavens—but the gun barrel twisted in a strange fashion and became inoperable. Then the second, third, and fourth Israeli tanks also tried to fire at the girl, and their gun barrels also twisted and became inoperable. As this was happening, the Palestinian gunmen tried to fire at the Israelis with automatic weapons, but the barrels of their weapons also twisted strangely. There were malfunctions of every weapon used at the site that day. After two full minutes of such inconsequential militance, both sides retreated.

A crowd of confused and delighted onlookers gathered in the square. The little girl and her mother went home.

In the newspapers the next day, there were varying accounts of what had happened. Some merely reported that there had been a skirmish in the Old City, from which both sides had withdrawn for strategic reasons, and no one had been hurt. Others reported on the simultaneous weapons malfunctions. One report told of the bravery of a little girl facing down the tanks—along with a photograph—but this account had limited circulation and there was no follow-up. In a larger view, this incident was important for what *didn't* happen. Since no one was killed on either side, neither Israelis nor Palestinians felt a need for reprisal, and so the fragile peace could continue.

In none of the circles of world leaders was there any mention of a small girl in a wheelchair standing up to a column of Israeli tanks. Her participation in this sequence of events, if known, was believed to be mere coincidence, and nothing more.

CHAPTER TWO

Garden of Eden

U pon returning to her home after the tank incident, the little girl did not rest. There were people who wanted to meet her and photograph her, but there were other things on her mind. She whispered something to her adoptive mother (which itself was remarkable), and Maya rolled her eyes upward, with a smile.

An hour later, a man named Joseph drove up to the front door of the merchant's home in a old black car. The little girl and her mother got in. The three of them drove off, as others watched and wondered.

It is unknown how this car and its driver and passengers crossed the border into Jordan, and then into Iraq. Normally, in this age of terror, people needed passports and other documents attesting to a legitimate purpose and an unblemished past. Certainly the driver must have been well-connected, for he not only knew the roads, but the right things to say at the checkpoints. The two women with him would not have the outward appearance of being a threat, but in this day and age one never knew. They might be insurgents planning to blow themselves up for a cause. Or they might be visiting relatives, or going to a funeral. As it turned out, the border guards were more concerned with the girl's wheelchair than with either her or her attendants. The guards searched the chair thoroughly for any sign of explosives, and let them pass.

Iraq has often been called the cradle of civilization. The city of Ur dates back to at least 3500 B.C., and was said to be near the Bible's Garden of Eden. In normal times, Iraq's thousands of ancient sites were visited regularly by archaeologists from around the world, but these were not normal times. As the car moved toward Baghdad, the bombed-out buildings and wrecked vehicles they passed pointed more toward Armageddon than a garden paradise. Was there a certain symmetry here for this region? Was this Land of the Beginning turning into the Final Reckoning for all mankind? Were Biblical prophesies of doom soon to be realized?

No one could know the thoughts of the little girl as the vehicle drove past the recent ruins of people's homes. She watched the scenes in silence, as did her adoptive mother and Joseph, the driver. The sun was setting as they approached Baghdad. There were occasional sounds of mortars in the distance, and of helicopter gunships and small-arms fire. No one knows where they spent that night. Presumably the driver had some connection and they found a home with beds.

There were further bombings that night—by Americans, by pro-American Iraqi soldiers, and by insurgents. And there were sirens, screams, and cries of anger and revenge, all heard by the little girl.

In the morning, deep in a basement of a building in the Green Zone in Central Baghdad, the American Command was having its daily meeting in the Operations Room. Officers from each of the American forces—the Army, Air Force, Navy, Marines, and National Guard—were present. They were working with the new Iraqi government to prepare a strategy to deal with the events of the night before. They decided to move two platoons from Zone A to Zone C—especially around the Italian Embassy. Five more tanks were needed just inside the Green Zone checkpoint, and three more support helicopters were to be in the northwestern sector from 04:15 to 07:30.

They were totally unprepared for the arrival of an unusual guest.

How she got there, no one knows. Indeed, there are many things in the life of the little girl which remain a mystery to this day. At any rate, she managed to open the door of the briefing room and move her wheelchair to within five feet of the main table. There were immediate shouts as three guards jumped on top of her and brought her and her wheelchair crashing to the floor. Meanwhile, the commanding officers had ducked under tables and chairs for cover, believing that this was another of the suicide attacks they had come to expect in this hostile land.

The guards searched the girl and her wheelchair for explosive devices. Finding none, they picked up the little creature and began to drag her out of the room. The officers peeked out from behind their respective covers to catch a glimpse of this anomaly in their lives. Just before the guards took the little girl from the room and she disappeared from their sight, she managed to speak—and they all heard—one word, in perfect English: "Out!"

Within minutes, the command room was back to normal, with phones ringing, data being entered in computers, and men poring over maps like hungry lions on the prowl. The interruption of the little girl became a distant memory for most, while for others it was a joke. There was some scolding of the guards who had allowed the girl to get that far, and pledges that such an intrusion would never happen again.

The little girl was taken in her wheelchair to a dimly lit room, where she stared at a cadre of angry interrogators who were well-trained in the art of extracting information from suspects. For forty-five minutes, the steely men tried to pry out anything they could about her life.

One of them tried to pinch her tiny cheeks, hard, and found sudden paralysis in both of his hands. Another tried to kick her withered legs and lost the use of his right foot. A third tried to grope her private parts while licking his tongue. He found that his fingers had ceased to function.

The five men were furious at first, and then fearful that they had encountered some kind of demonic power that was stronger than them. They decided to release the girl immediately and concoct some kind of story about her being rescued by a gang of twenty terrorists whom they had bravely fought off, saving the high officers from certain death. They were given medals for their heroism, and thought that this little girl had forever disappeared from their lives.

The next day, a peculiar sickness appeared in the ranks of American soldiers stationed in Iraq. It first struck the soldiers' stomachs with nausea and then their heads with a terrible fever. It was reported in Baghdad, and then in Fallujah, Kirkuk, Mosul, Basra, and Najah. Scores, hundreds, thousands, and then tens of thousands of American soldiers were moved to sick bay and flown out of the country for treatment in Germany or at home. They appeared to recover over time in the "good old American air," but the military consequence of this epidemic was significant. As U.S. troops were flown away, other Coalition members became worried that America was abandoning them. They began to withdraw their troops, too.

As the U.S. President and his advisers pondered this turn of events, they agreed that the best course of action, as always, was to hide the truth from everyone and make up something that would make Americans proud. They designed a complete cover-up of the sickness which had afflicted so many American soldiers, and announced that Iraq was suddenly "free and stable" and that American troops would no longer be needed there. Within a few weeks, Iraq was free of all foreign soldiers. And then, incredibly, Iraqis of all faiths came together for the first time in many years to try to rebuild their country.

This, the President claimed, had been the plan all along.

CHAPTER THREE

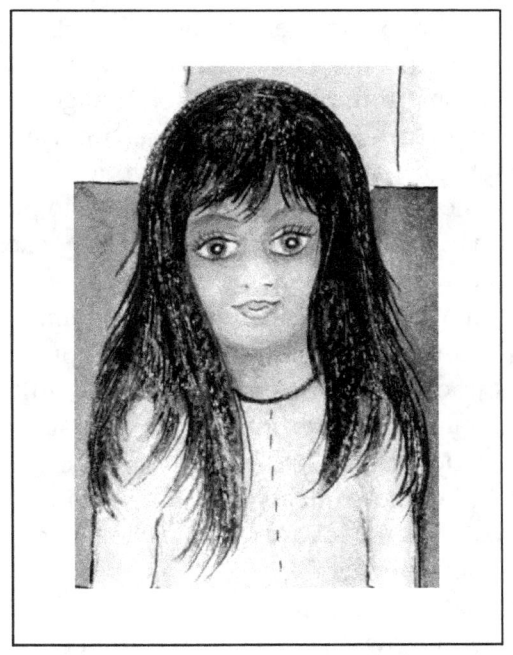

Revelation

At the turn of the twenty-first century, it was natural for most people to view world leaders with a measure of skepticism. This was particularly true of the U.S. President. For him to suddenly withdraw all American troops from Iraq was inconsistent with his many speeches stating that American forces would stay there "until Iraqis can defend themselves against the insurgents." Many believed that something more had to be happening. A number of theories were developed.

One theory was that America was withdrawing its troops from Iraq in order to use them somewhere else—like Iran or North Korea. Another was that there was a more sinister plan to use these troops to implement major changes at home. Still another was that the President's born-again Christianity was leading him toward some kind of apocalyptic plan.

Naturally, there were journalists who tried to pry deeper into the details of what had happened recently. They carefully examined the curious report of a sudden weapons dysfunction in Jerusalem. When they asked the Israeli and Palestinian leaders about this, none of them admitted to any such weaponry problem. Several reporters tracked down the account of the little girl defying the enormous tanks. They examined the photograph, and went to her home in Jerusalem. They were unsuccessful in locating the girl herself, but they did talk to the merchant in whose home she had lived, and to the teacher at her school for the deaf. They stopped there, sensing that this was an inconsequential dead end.

Other journalists carefully reviewed the events in Iraq leading up to the withdrawal of troops. They uncovered numerous accounts of sickness; and one asked the President, at a rare press conference, "Isn't it true that the sickness of so many American soldiers was a major reason for the withdrawal of American forces from Iraq?"

The President had a ready answer for this question. He grinned and said, "Look, these are the finest fightin' men in the world . . . and gals too—as we all know, gals can be really tough, too." (The President cackled alone.) "Look, do you honestly think that a little flu or sickness can bother these fellas?

If you do, you don't know the United States military. I rest my case."

This answer was unconvincing to many journalists, who suspected more than coincidence in the sudden sickness and subsequent withdrawal. They probed further, and asked hundreds of troops how they got sick and what they thought might have caused it.

One of the reporters stumbled onto one of the guards who had attended the curious Operations Room meeting. The guard rambled on for half an hour about the battle plans under discussion. Then, in a moment of carelessness, he mentioned, as a side note, the little girl in the wheelchair.

The reporter questioning him couldn't believe his ears. "Wait a minute," he whispered, so as not to attract attention. "Could you go over that again?"

The guard repeated the story of the little girl entering the war room in her wheelchair, and told how she had spoken the word, "Out." just before being taken away. The guard then described how the specialists had interrogated her, and how three of them had been injured before she was released to the street.

The reporter did not rush off immediately to write his story and release it as the greatest scoop of the year. He calmly asked the guard if any photographs had been taken of the young girl. The guard said "sure," and said it would probably take a couple of days to track them down.

Two days later, the guard brought three photographs showing the little girl with the withered legs shackled to her wheelchair and enduring intense cross-examination from her five interrogators. Promising anonymity, the reporter paid the guard one thousand dollars and left with the photographs. He immediately went back to his hotel room, pulled out the picture of the girl facing the Israeli tanks, and compared them. They were a match!

The story broke the next day and made headlines all over the world. An enormous crowd assembled immediately at the Old Jerusalem home of the little girl, hoping to catch a glimpse of her, her mother, or the driver of the car. The merchant and school teacher were interviewed countless times, and a worldwide search was started to track down the three instant celebrities.

The story dominated the world news for several days. Arab newspapers not only hailed the little girl as the conqueror of the "Evil West," but also noted that her birth mother, Hagar, bore the name of "The Mother of Islam." It had been so long since Arabs had defeated the western powers in anything military that there was rejoicing in the streets, with guns fired into the air, as was the custom in many parts of the Arab world.

The girl was said to be a direct descendant of Mohammed. She was compared to the mighty Saladin, whose army had turned away Richard the Lion Heart's army at the gates of Jerusalem a thousand years earlier. Stories were told of how this little girl single-handedly brought the "Western devils" (America, Britain, and Israel) to their knees. A few of the stories were true. Most were not. It didn't matter. Muslims worldwide were deliriously proud.

Totally different groups in Asia, Europe, and the Americas became devotees of the little girl because of her effective use of nonviolence to achieve peace.

Buddhists, perhaps in violation of their own creed, became excited about the girl's natural affinity to their leader. Hindus compared her to Gandhi, who had driven the British out of India with a simple handful of salt.

Americans compared her to Martin Luther King Jr., whose peaceful protests brought equality to many African Americans.

Children identified with the little girl's bravery in standing up to foolish adults.

Handicapped people felt especially empowered.

And many liberal thinkers who had lost all hope of decency in the future of mankind, began to see this little girl as the answer to their prayers.

On the other side, there were many who felt instant hate for this little creature. She was a threat to Israel, to America, and to all they held dear. How could she be trusted to bring about major change? She was only seven. She had no education, no experience in the real world. Who was her God? What were her values?

Did she claim to be the Messiah? This was very important. If she did, then she was a threat to Christianity, Judaism, Islam, and every other self-respecting religion.

Some viewed her as an epitome of darkness and evil, who needed to be killed in order to save the world.

CHAPTER FOUR

Allah is Merciful

While news organizations of the world were conducting a vast search for the enigmatic child, the slight shadows of three figures on camels moved along white sand dunes beneath a crescent moon. Stars filled the sky, and a gentle breeze stroked the travelers as they made their way westward. The little girl was smiling as she watched her camel lurch ahead, step by step, in a steady gait. For this instant in time, she had forgotten the problems of the planet, and was basking in the glory of the heavens.

Since Ishmael, son of Hagar and first-born son of Abraham, kicked the sand and opened the spring of Zemzem long ago, Mecca had been a Holy City. Muslims from all over the world were commanded to make the pilgrimage here at least once in a lifetime, while all others ("infidels") were commanded to stay away.

As the three riders approached the city, they saw large temples rising above houses mostly made of clay. They passed through one set of gates and noticed the growing numbers of people as they came closer to the Holy Shrine of the *Kaaba*. At one point they tied their camels to a palm tree. After the little girl's wheelchair was brought to the ground, she was placed in it and moved forward while the other two walked behind. The crowds grew thicker, and the faces more and more radiant, as people approached the shrine.

At a short distance from the *Kaaba*, there was a building called the *Ihram* with fountains of water where devotees were supposed to bathe, change into white clothes, and remove their shoes. From this place on to the *Kaaba*, there was little conversation or other normal sounds. The people were praying to Allah and feeling touched by His spirit. The little girl turned off her vehicle's motor and wheeled her chair along by the strength of her tiny arms.

As the three pilgrims moved into the building encircling the *Kaaba*, they were unrecognized by anyone around them. They passed through the enclosed area (the *Turaca*) where Hagar was said to have run back and forth seven times after her son Ishmael had found water. As the three figures moved into the open court-yard, where masses of people were circling the *Kaaba* seven times before touching the Holy Stone of Abraham (passed down from Adam), a small boy noticed the wheelchair. He approached the little girl, looked into her eyes, and recognized her from the many photographs which had been sent out around the world. His eyes bulged and he poked his companion, who also looked.

Soon there were hundreds, and then thousands, of pilgrims who were aware of the presence of a very important person in the Arab world. There was no pause in the pace of the crowd movement. There were no shouts, no cheers, or other noises to indicate that anything special was happening. But it did not take long for almost everyone in the area of the *Kaaba* to know that the famous little girl who had stood up to the western world was in their midst. The security guards immediately took notice and called the king, who left a banquet to come to the *Kaaba* in person.

The circling of the *Kaaba* does not happen fast. At any one time there are likely to be hundreds of thousands, and sometimes more than a million people, all moving in the same direction. It is done with order and reverence.

The three special pilgrims moved forward for almost two hours, getting closer and closer to the large black square rock called the *Kaaba*. When at last they reached the part of the *Kaaba* in which the Black Stone of Abraham protruded for each pilgrim to touch, they paused for a moment to sense the special spirit of the occasion. By this time, thousands of other pilgrims had turned slightly to watch the little girl touch the Black Stone.

At that moment, a large white-gowned man stood up next to them and yelled in Arabic for all to hear:

"Praise be to Mohammed! Praise be to Al Qaeda! Allah is great!"

He raised a large jeweled sword into the air and brought it down with all his might onto the tiny neck of the little girl in the wheelchair.

What happened next is unclear. It all occurred in a split

second of adrenaline and blurred vision. Even security camera tapes which were examined later failed to reveal all the details.

Some say that the little girl reached up and grabbed the sword before it could find its mark. Others say that the man lost his balance and fell to the ground. Still others say that an invisible shield protected the girl from the attacker. At any rate, when it was over, the little girl and her would-be assassin were left untouched, and the assassin was weeping on the ground before her.

The little girl then picked up the large sword, broke it in two, and dropped it on the ground. In a soft voice that for some reason echoed throughout the courtyard, she said, "Allah is merciful." Then she put her tiny hands around the man's head, and hugged him.

He sobbed.

A short time later, she, Maya, and Joseph went across the courtyard to the footstep of Mohammed carved from stone, crossed down to a lower level to drink holy water from the *Zemzem* spring, and left the *Kaaba*.

Among the witnesses of this event, from their safe spot on top of the wall above the *Kaaba*, were the King of Saudi Arabia and fifteen of his brothers. After returning to their local palace, they ordered that copies of the security videotape be given to the media of the world.

The effect on parts of the planet was enormous. The sight of the killer trying to behead the little girl, the "deific" intervention, the "miracle" of the girl breaking the sword in two, and her immediate call for mercy—all these sent strong messages to many kinds of people.

More people of the world began to see her as a religious figure, full of miracles and worthy of worship. Of course, journalists and TV personalities wanted to interview her and make fortunes. The paparazzi factor was acute. Many people were entranced, as they wondered what she might do next. And sadly, there were still many who believed her to be the devil and wanted her dead.

Perhaps the greatest effect was on the Al Qaeda organization.

No longer could it seriously claim to be either righteous or powerful. Its numbers dwindled to insignificance, and its leaders were transformed from Islamic heroes to has-been zealots.

Publicly the U.S. President hailed the little girl as "a symbol of peace in the world." Privately, he ordered "every God-Damned spy we have to find out who she is and what she's up to!" In his heart of hearts, the President knew that this little girl was taking away his greatest asset—world terrorism, and that without this nemesis to scare the American people, his political power was in jeopardy.

CHAPTER FIVE

The Prodigal Dwarf

R ich Barton was an achondroplasmian dwarf, which means that he had very short limbs. In all other respects he was normal, or above normal. But his dwarfness, superficial as it should have been, dwarfed all his other features. Going to the supermarket meant being stared at, every time. The big kids would whisper and point, and the little kids would yell things like, "Hey Mommie! Look at the funny man!"

At an early age, he began to tell himself, "Rich, get over it. You're a dwarf. So what? Everybody has problems, and at least yours doesn't hurt or keep you from doing anything. Well, all right, so you're probably not going to play in the NBA—or maybe you will. Who knows? Don't set limits. You can do anything. You're just a dwarf. That's all."

Of course, stores weren't the only places where dwarfs had trouble. There was the men's shower, the dance floor, pushy crowds, big stairs and, well, just about anywhere where people weren't sitting down. Ah, sitting down! Now that was the level playing field—where dwarfs could be like everyone else.

When he wasn't dwelling on his dwarfness, Rich was a 62-year-old Professor of Anthropology at a university near Ashland, Oregon. He lived with his Brazilian wife, Maria, and their six-year-old son, Peter, in a spectacular home overlooking the Rogue River.

Dwarfness aside, Rich had led a life of adventure—seeking out war zones, primitive cultures, and people with interesting tales to tell. He'd collected degrees like stamps: Anthropology, Journalism, Law and Social Welfare. He spoke seven languages fluently and had a range of friends which included cannibals in Brazil, Pygmies in the Congo, monks in Tibet, and fellow magicians throughout the world.

One day, the Fourteenth Dalai Lama of Tibet invited Rich into his living room in Dharamsala for an intimate talk. "Your Holiness," a nervous Rich said at the start of the interview, "I really appreciate your giving me this time, and, uh, treating me as if I were normal."

"My friend," said the Dalai Lama, looking deep into his

eyes, "your body is a gift. It opens the hearts of others and leaves your ego behind. You are truly blessed."

Rich pondered these words every day in the years to follow. A gift? Well, maybe in some ways. But would he trade this "gift" for a normal body? In a dwarf's heartbeat! Meanwhile his mother, Kay, referred to him with sarcastic affection as "my prodigal dwarf," while prodding him to return home and "act more normal."

Rich's life changed, twenty minutes before midnight, one New Year's Eve. He met Maria, a Brazilian woman who saw through to Rich's real person and had no problem with his "condition." They were married and moved to Ashland, Oregon "to get away from the problems of urban America." Peter was born two years later, bringing Rich "immense joy in every second of every day."

Meanwhile, Rich fed his mind by teaching a variety of courses at the university level. He shared stories of his travels with his students, and talked freely about what he described as "the sad state of the world." From South Asia's polluted skies to North Africa's expanding deserts, the Middle East's unending religious tension, South America's growing poverty and North America's frenzied consumption, the human race was headed on a precipitous course toward extinction. He tried not to be too negative in front of these young students full of dreams, but he couldn't help it. From his own experience, the future looked bleak.

When Rich Barton read the article on the little girl's appearance in Israel, he was at his home computer. He recalled the day two years ago when he had viewed a similar tank showdown from the window of his hotel in Old Jerusalem. He remembered having thought about how it would be nice if all the guns simply ceased to function. When he saw the photograph of the scene with the little girl, he was amazed to discover that the picture looked like it had been taken from that same hotel room.

When Rich read about the little girl's appearance in the

Operations Room in Baghdad, he knew instantly where that room was, because he'd been there, too, on that same trip two years ago. In that room, he'd thought wistfully of how nice it would be if the American soldiers just went away and left the Iraqi people to work out their differences in peace.

When he read about the recent incident at the *Kaaba*, Rich recalled his own visit to Mecca on that same trip, just after the stop in Baghdad. Dressed in Arab garb, armed with a false Palestinian passport, speaking fluent Arabic, and with an apparently harmless dwarf's body, he had no trouble gaining entrance to the holy shrine. At the very moment that he touched the legendary stone, he had a vision of a little girl being attacked there by a man with a sword.

This was beginning to feel creepy.

The ties between Rich and the little girl might be attributed to mere coincidence, or to a failing mind. But it might also be something much bigger, and more bizarre.

"Daddy," said his son Peter, who was looking at the pictures. "This girl looks like she's my age."

"Yes, I know. I think she is your age."

"Is she going to be all right?"

"I hope so, sweetie."

Wide-awake in bed in the early hours of the morning, Rich recalled the next stop on that trip he had taken on that trip two years ago: Darfur.

CHAPTER SIX

Blessed are the Meek

The Janjaweed were a gang of mostly young male thugs who had terrorized the Darfur region of Western Sudan for years. They traveled by camel or truck and wore black robes and masks. They rode into poor black African villages with guns and machetes, killed the men and children, and then raped and killed the women.

They claimed to be "men of Allah" purging the world of the evils of black people and of those with religions other than their own. In reality, they were sadists who delighted in the screams and suffering of people who were helpless.

The village of Majengo was struck late at night. Two hundred very poor black Christians heard the shouts from a distance. Those who were strong enough tried to flee, but most of the villagers were too old, too young, too sick, or too weak, to run. They huddled together on the dirt inside their mud huts. They held their Bibles and prayed to a god who never came. In their last moments before the strike of the machetes, they asked for a better life in the world beyond.

As the sun rose on Majengo the next morning, more than one hundred carcasses lay in the huts and on the ground. Another twenty villagers were in the last throes of life, lying in their own blood, vomit, and excrement, writhing in pain.

Risking death, a group of ten survivors quietly moved through sandy thickets and re-entered their village. They knew what to expect. Their faces were grim, and they were unable to hold back tears as they found the bodies of their mothers, fathers, sons, daughters and others. They had a little dirty water to pour in the mouths of their loved ones, but no food, no medicine, nothing else. For many miles around there was no help. The world had forgotten them. Their lives were pure agony, and no one cared.

By the middle of the morning, most of the other survivors had returned to the village in a state of shock. They held the bodies of their bloodied relatives in their arms and wept. They knew the Janjaweed might return that day, but they didn't care. In the hot sun, they buried as many of the bodies as they could, gathered in one space near an open fire, and sat in tears and silence.

Late in the afternoon, an unknown shape appeared on the horizon. The villagers grew tense as it came closer. They clutched their Bibles and prayed. They hugged each other, watching the shapes of three riders on camels come into view. They were not moving fast nor making threatening motions, as was customary for the Janjaweed. The villagers stared in amazement as they saw that two of the riders were women, one a small girl. The other was a man.

As the three riders approached, the villagers yelled at them in Arabic to go back, or go away—that their lives would be in danger here. The riders came into the village anyway. After the camels folded their legs to a kneeling position in their typically awkward fashion, two of the riders dismounted. The man opened a wheelchair for the small girl, and she was placed in it.

The air had the stench of death, vomit, and excrement. Flies were everywhere, clusters of buzzards were picking at some of the remains, and a hyena was howling, not far away.

One of the villagers asked the little girl, "Would you like some water? It's dirty, but it's all we have."

Instead of answering, the little girl, then the woman, and then the man, just hugged the survivors of last night's massacre. The strange man opened a bag of cooked rice and a container of fresh water, and the villagers devoured it gratefully. There were some smiles—the first seen in that village for a long time.

More shapes appeared on the horizon, becoming a large cloud of dust with angry shouts and the sight of arms waving swords. This time the villagers stayed together. They held each other's hands, chanted prayers, and marveled that the three strangers stayed with them to die.

What happened next was related in many different forms by the villagers who were witnesses. As the Janjaweed came to within fifty meters of the poor villagers, the little girl said one word to them in Arabic: "*Khef!*" (Stop!)

The attackers did not stop. Instead they rode directly at the group with machetes raised for the slaughter. And, as each rider came to within ten meters of the gathering, he simply disappeared, along with his machete and camel.

One after the other, ten, twenty, fifty riders, machetes, and camels. Gone.

The villagers stared in disbelief. Was this a dream? Were they in Heaven? After several minutes, they realized that indeed they were still alive in their village, and, at least for this instant, were safe.

Then, slowly, each of the ten villagers reached out to touch the little girl. There was no need to say thank you, no need to speak to describe their feelings. Just touching a part of her frail body was enough to express the reverence they felt. It did not take long for this story to reach the outside world. Someone walked a mile down a road and met someone on horseback, who went to a town that had a radio. There was mention of a little girl in a wheelchair.

Within a short time, more than five thousand journalists, politicians, relief workers and others appeared in the area to learn more about the curious incident in the desert, and to find the little girl and her friends, and, peripherally, to help the villagers.

In the aftermath, there were rumors of other Janjaweed riders simply disappearing, mere moments before they could strike their victims. Reports of this reached still other Janjaweed gangs, who retreated back to where they came, in Southern Sudan. In these circumstances, they became God-fearing men and no longer dared to wreak havoc upon anyone, even their wives and girlfriends.

Once again, the report of the little girl's activities made news around the world. She was becoming a cult heroine, despite the fact that few had seen her and many suspected that she was a creation of the media. Speculation abounded. The headlines inspired nations and individuals to send massive amounts of aid to build refugee camps, and to provide clean water, food, and medical care for the millions of Africans suffering in this region.

*****

At his desk in the Oval Office, the U.S. President turned to his closest aide. "I'd like to invite this little girl over to my ranch at Crawford," he said. "I think it's about time we had a little chat."

At his desk overlooking the Rogue River, Rich Barton recalled spending a sleepless night two years ago with the people of Majengo. Every noise in the distance might have been the Janjaweed, but they didn't come that night. He remembered having a nightmare about them, in which they were about to slice his head off when he awoke. He thought—maybe wished—that each Janjaweed warrior, before striking a victim, would just disappear.

Now something like that had happened again. Just like his dreams, or wishes, had come true in Jerusalem, Baghdad and Mecca.

Richard Barton waited until after Peter was asleep before inviting Maria out to their favorite chairs on the deck. "Honey, can you keep a secret?"

"Of course," she said with a grin. "I love secrets."

"Well this one's not like most secrets," he said in a serious tone. "It's . . . well, crazy, and it seems to be happening to me."

"What's the matter," Maria cooed. "Are you thinking of that little girl in the wheelchair again? Should I be jealous?"

"Maria," he replied, "What I'm going to tell you cannot be shared with anyone else on the planet. Ever! Do you understand?"

"Yes, dear." She, too, was serious now, realizing that Rich was tense and troubled.

He told her about each incident in turn. She listened in silence. At last she said, "Sweetie, I don't know what to say. It seems so unreal. Somehow I can't believe that it's actually happening."

"But it is," he replied, "and to me. And the question now is, 'What do I do about it?' Do I go to the place I went next on that trip—Uganda. and try to meet with her? Do I just let things happen? Or do I have some special responsibility to warn people, and maybe take some action?"

"Maybe you should report this to the government."

"I've thought of that. But the truth is that I can't stand this administration. That would be like consorting with the enemy. Besides, they'd follow our every move and make our lives miserable. No, that's why we've both got to keep this a secret from everyone we know."

CHAPTER SEVEN

The Miracle

The small village of Uchumi, in Northeastern Uganda, had seen its share of trouble. In the days of Idi Amin, his soldiers came there frequently to pick out young girls for brief pleasure. Sometimes the girls were spared afterward, but more often they were fed to crocodiles in the nearby gorge below Murchison Falls.

When Idi Amin went north into exile in Sudan, the village was beset by roaming bands who were little more than mercenaries for hire. Aside from their perennial appetite for instant genital gratification, these mercenaries recruited young boys and girls to serve in such capacities as gun bearers, cooks, spies, and long-term sex slaves. The older people in Uchumi tried to hide their young girls and boys as best they could, but the villagers lived in constant fear of kidnapping, rape and death.

Over the years, the marauders' visits became less frequent, and another problem appeared: the AIDS virus. Despite the new government's best efforts to warn its citizens, this disease had infected two thirds of the five hundred people in the village. Worse, those infected tended to be between the ages of twelve and thirty, and were the hardest workers. Without their ploughing the fields, hunting antelope, cooking manioc and gathering firewood, the village's basic needs could not be met.

In the old days, the village of Uchumi had taken great pride in its school, with its large brick structure, its wooden beams, chairs and tables, and corrugated roof. The school even had a generator for electricity for adult night classes. There was a brief period when students of high school age talked of their ambitions to become teachers, doctors and engineers. A couple of the village youths won scholarships to go to college in Europe, and one went all the way to the University of Iowa in America. Others had a different desire—to leave the village, make lots of money, and send it back home to help their families.

This all changed with the coming of the virus. Since there were few cultural rules restricting intercourse, AIDS found its way into the blood of more than fifty young people in the first year. It took several more years for the villagers to truly believe the teachings about how the virus was transmitted. By that time, it was too late. The school, once an object of pride, became a hospital for the terminally ill. The home of the headmaster, for lack of an alternative, became a morgue.

The three large former schoolrooms in the hospital were divided into the stages of the disease. The first had twenty beds for those with open wounds from *Karposi sarcoma*, or who had diarrhea, or whose stomachs retched every hour or so, or who coughed constantly—but they could walk to a nearby outhouse by themselves, most of the time. The second room was reserved for those who were not ambulatory, but who could still talk and make some sense. The third room was reserved for those on the brink of death—who had little left of body or mind, and for whom a priest stood by to give the last rites. At each instant of a new death, an effort was made to move the corpse to the morgue quickly so that the putrid smell and the sound of the wailers were kept at a distance.

On this day, Mary Njathi was in charge of the hospital. She was in good health for her fifty-five years, and needed all of her strength to withstand the moaning, sobbing, constant complaining, anger, depression, and hopelessness of the people she loved most in the world. She knew that she needed to be empathetic, but she also needed to keep from going crazy and jumping off the nearby "Rock of Death," which had become the preferred place for the ultimate relief of suffering and despair. Her husband, her five oldest children, and seven of her grandchildren had already died from the virus, and now her youngest grandchild—only three years old—had just been moved from Room One to Room Two.

Mary was washing vomit from the face and clothes of her youngest grandchild, thinking how much she loved this creature, and feeling the tears drip down her face onto the child's cheeks, when another attendant called her, "Mary, someone is coming." But Mary's feelings were totally focused on her grandchild, so she did not look up for a while. When she did, it was with a perfunctory sense of some other chore to perform, or perhaps a new patient.

When Mary at last went to the door and looked, she saw the figures of three people—a man, a woman, and a child in a wheelchair. She had no idea what was happening, but she watched as they approached. As the strangers came to the door of the second room, nothing was said. The little girl, with tears streaming down her face, reached up and embraced Mary for a long time. At some point, the embrace ended, and Mary led the little girl into Room Two to the cot on which lay her youngest grandchild.

The little girl in the wheelchair reached out with her small hands and placed them on this child's forehead, where scabs and sores were already beginning to claim her for the life beyond. Child to child, energy passed between them. Since the witnesses were few, it is not known how long they stayed that way. But, over time, the younger child's scabs and sores disappeared and she opened her eyes wide.

Mary hugged her grandchild, and the little girl in the wheelchair went on to the next patient, a young man. There was the same laying of hands on his forehead, and over time the same disappearance of the marks which had branded him as a victim of the virus. The little girl went to each patient in Room Two, one by one, and relieved their visual symptoms. Then she went to Room Three, and did the same, one by one. And then she went to Room One, and did the same.

It should be said that these patients did not fully recover immediately. They lay on their cots, weak and exhausted, for days afterward, still coughing and retching occasionally; but they all gradually grew stronger and began to eat and hold down their food. And the smiles returned, both to them and to their loved ones outside of the schoolhouse. None of them died from the virus.

As word spread of "the miracle," others with the virus were brought to the schoolhouse, and there was the same laying on of hands, and the same slow, steady relief of symptoms. The villagers rejoiced in the way they knew best—singing church songs and dancing in colorful costumes with hips swaying. The three-room schoolhouse was transformed from a place of suffering to a place of healing and joy.

People with other medical problems—headaches, snake bites, machete cuts, appendicitis, and cancer—began to arrive at the door of the schoolhouse, but the little girl in the wheelchair was not ready to cure all ailments. Amidst imploring and then anger by both victims and their relatives, these people were turned away. The little girl in the wheelchair was treating only those with the AIDS virus.

When the media heard of this new activity of the little girl in the wheelchair, there was a stampede to the small village of Uchumi. Helicopters with cameras whirred overhead, scaring many villagers who thought that new bands of marauders might have arrived. Large trucks came with generators to power cameras and send electronic images off to distant viewers. Money was passed freely to those who had stories to tell of the recent events, and foreign reporters pushed their way through the local crowds to try to film the little girl herself.

Then suddenly, as if by magic, the little girl in the wheelchair, Maya, and Joseph disappeared. But the most important part of this story was what happened next.

All across the planet, people with the AIDS virus began to feel better. Their symptoms subsided, and then disappeared. Within a few weeks the virus itself disappeared. There was widespread rejoicing, particularly in those communities which had the most AIDS victims. Medical conventions sprang up as experts tried to understand what had just happened. It didn't make sense, and yet there it was.

At the White House, a beaming President called a press conference and said, "My fellow Americans, and others throughout the world, I am very proud to announce a major piece of good news. Through the hard work of American scientists, and you, the taxpayers who have given so generously, we have succeeded in defeating the HIV virus. No more must people suffer at the hands of this great disorder. No more will this disorder bring backbreaking pain and discomfiture to millions lying at home or on the streets. No more, because this disorder has gone the way of the woolly mammoth, of the Napoleonic war, and of terrorists around the world. It's gone, terminated, bye-bye!"

One of the reporters asked, "Mr. President, can you tell us exactly how American scientists cured this disease?"

"Look," he answered, "I'm no scientist. As you know I only got Cs in college—when I was lucky." (He laughed.) "You'll have to get the details from the fellas who know these things."

"But we have asked them," came the follow-up question, "and they say they don't know."

"Look, all I know is that America has the finest scientists in the world, and that they've been working on this thing for years . . . *years!* And they've come up with all sorts of pills and, what's it called . . . uh, cocktails, yeah cocktails, to treat folks with AIDS, so you put this all together and . . . look! It's only logical. They've been working on a cure, the thing's been cured, and—well what do you think? That the thing cured itself?"

The next reporter asked, "What about the little girl in the wheelchair? Did she have anything to do with this? Have you heard about her? Do you have any comment on this?"

"Yes, of course I've heard," said the President. "I've heard all about this little girl, and I can tell you that I, too, know what it's like to be a parent in today's world. I know because I have my own two little girls. And don't let anybody tell you that parenting is easy, because it's not." He snickered and added, "You, over there in the back row, you know what I mean! Now, next question . . ."

In his office, Rich Barton read the latest reports from Uganda and then at AIDS centers around the world. He recalled spending time at Uchumi with Mary Njathi. One night he had even told her how he wished this whole AIDS epidemic "would just go away." But at the time it was just musing—a distant dream that had nothing whatsoever to do with reality. And now it had happened.

What if things were as they were now appearing to be—that he, Rich Barton, through the powers of this little creature, could somehow make all of his dreams come true? What if Rich Barton could transform the world, bit by bit, into the kind of place he had always hoped it would be? It was like being a god, or *the* god! Such endless potential, and responsibility, and mistakes— yes, he was sure to make mistakes. Good grief!

CHAPTER EIGHT

The Firmament

A t 1:45 in the morning, Rich Barton was sitting in a chair on his back porch in Oregon, above the Rogue River, looking up at the heavens. *Except for the moon and a couple of planets,* he thought, *not one of those little lights in the sky is really there. They're just ghosts of stars that used to be there, but which have moved on to some other location. In some ways they're like life on this planet—remote, mysterious, unknowable.*

When people asked him about his own religion, his preferred answer was, "I believe in the incomprehensibility of God."

As a teacher of Comparative Religion, Rich had often described the history and basic concepts of "The Big Five." Hinduism was always first, with its craziness—millions of gods and goddesses constantly changing color, shape and species. Vishnu's ten incarnations included a fish, a turtle, a boar and a lion. The ninth incarnation was Buddha, and the tenth was a metallic creature called Kalki who rode a white horse and reorganized the social order of humankind. Was this little girl a kind of Kalki? It made as much sense as anything else.

The trouble with Hinduism, Rich thought, is that it's too passive. Humans are relegated to a *dharma,* or predetermined mission in life, which they have to accept. In the *Bhagavad Gita,* the poor warrior Arjuna wanted so much to avoid leading his army into battle against his cousins. But Lord Krishna directed him to follow his *dharma* and go to war anyway. In this setting, Rich would have disobeyed Lord Krishna and refused to fight.

Judaism, Rich thought, is problematic for several reasons. First, it's limited to people who were Jewish (or children of Jewish mothers). And second, the Old Testament was so full of violence and retribution that it conflicted with Rich's pacifist principles. A standard essay question on Rich's final exam was, "How can you reconcile the Old Testament's god of wrath with the New Testament's god of peace and forgiveness? Should these be viewed as two separate gods, and two separate religions?"

Rich had vivid memories of living on Israel's Kibbutz Galed, and of talking for hours with old timers Yitrzrak and Michael while they were picking peaches in the *matayin* (orchards). "You may notice," Yitrzrak told him once, "that there are no rabbis on this kibbutz. The German founders of Galed—myself included, were so horrified by the Nazi holocaust that we concluded that if there was a Jewish god, He was either impotent or He didn't care about His people. Nothing else can explain what happened to our families in those years."

Rich thought, *What if this little girl from Jerusalem had appeared in 1940? What would she have done then?*

Buddhism was foreign to Rich until he spent a year in India and Nepal. His introduction to it came through his guide, Lakpa, on a thirty-day trek to the base camp of Mount Everest. Lakpa was young and strong. He had led two successful summits of *Sagarmatha*, as the Sherpas called Everest. He was always smiling, and yet he was born to serve. "Your happiness is my happiness," he used to say; and he meant it. The concept was so totally different from the American creed of independence that Rich puzzled over it for a long time.

When Rich arranged for a meeting with the Dalai Lama at the end of his trip to India, he didn't know what to expect. He knew that Buddhists didn't actually worship a god the way other religions did. "God" was more of a concept of letting go of attachments and of feeling compassion for everyone and everything in the universe. And yet, for a full forty-five minutes in Dharamsala, Rich photographed Tibetan devotees being blessed by this "Fourteenth Incarnation" of the original Dalai Lama. These people treated the Dalai Lama like a god. Rich watched as the Dalai Lama touched each of them gently on the hands and head to give them a blessing. And, after the blessings, the Dalai Lama had taken Rich's hand and held it while leading Rich into his nearby living room. As they talked together, the Dalai Lama grinned and laughed and was totally accommodating to Rich's needs. He answered Rich's many questions in the same manner as Lakpa had served Rich for thirty days on the trek to Mount Everest. Amazing!

Christianity was in Rich's heritage on all sides of his family.

He remembered going to the Episcopal Church of St. Mary the Virgin in San Francisco for the first ten years of his life. He found the organ music creepy, and resented having to sit in a pew in his dark wool suit when he'd rather be playing in his jeans in the fresh air of a nearby park. But he also loved the lines of Matthew 5:

> *Blessed are the poor in spirit, for theirs is the king-dom of heaven.*
>
> *Blessed are they that mourn, for they shall be comforted.*
>
> *Blessed are the meek, for they shall inherit the earth . . .*

Now here was a man, a god, a philosophy, that Rich could embrace!

But the more Rich learned of the faith parts of his church (Mary's virgin birth, Jesus being the son of God, and his as-cension into Heaven), the harder it became for Rich to accept Christianity. It became still harder as Rich studied the history of this religion—the Dark Ages of the Roman Empire, the Spanish Inquisition, the brutal conquest of the Americas, and the many wars fought in the name of Jesus. Rich recalled George Bernard Shaw's statement, "The only trouble with Christianity is that it's never been tried." Rich would tell people that he tried to live by the basic principles of Jesus, but without the encumbrances of a particular church.

So how might the little girl be related to Christianity? Some Christians were already calling her a Messiah because she had been born near Bethlehem and had performed "miracles" on a larger scale than anyone in history. Healing the sick and helping the oppressed was a central part of Jesus' life. But she was not talking about a god. Indeed, she wasn't even talking! She was just doing a lot of crying and hugging. Seven years old was a lot younger than Jesus at thirty. And, unlike Jesus, crucifixion did not appear to be in her future.

Of the five major religions, Rich had found Islam the most difficult to understand. Mohammed was both a warrior and a man of mercy. Most Muslims were, at the same time, single-minded about their faith in Allah and deeply humble and compassionate in their daily lives. Rich recalled his first day in Amman, Jordan, when he was awakened in his hotel room by the sound of an Arabic chant blasting through loudspeakers to wake up the whole city. So disruptive, and yet so reverent.

Is the little girl really a Muslim? Rich wondered, *or was there some other purpose in her going to the sacred* Kaaba?

Rich finally dozed off in his chair at 3:30 am. Maria put a cover over him, and he slept soundly beneath the ghosts of stars.

CHAPTER NINE

The Book of Joan

Nesting eternally in the *Suite de Plaisir* of the Hotel Ritz in the heart of Paris, was a centenarian who was adored in Europe and ignored by the rest of the world. She boasted affairs with everyone from Picasso to Pope Pius XI, from Hemingway to Ho Chi Minh, and from Churchill to Degas, Faulkner, Hitler, Idi Amin, Johnson, Kennedy, Lennon, McCartney, Napoleon VI, Roosevelt, Schweitzer, Tiny Tim, U Thant, Valentino, several Williamses, Xerxes XXXV, Yanni and Zapata.

She lived by the maxim, "Make love, not war," and preached a gospel of diverting the testeronic male half of our population toward estrogen. Her writings used countless *noms de plume,* among them Jeanne d'Arc, Jeanne de Gaulle, Jeanne Paul Sartre, Jeanne Valjean and Jeanne de Buisson. The prenom sufficed for her many readers.

Endeavoring to translate from her French to my English is like trying to serve salad without dressing, *ou fromage sans vin.* Nevertheless, with apologies to Jeanne and her many followers, here is an attempt on a poem from one of her recent books:

The Little Girl and the Lost Planet
by Jeanne Le Monde

After a hundred years,
and more than my share of tears,
I find the human race
to be a sad disgrace.

The menfolk wave their swords,
pretending they are Lords,
And kill to bring us peace,
in Jesus 'name—Oh please!

The rich keep getting richer,
and the poor shall live in pain
For as long as Bible bearers
ignore Matthew's refrain.

The land is being raped
by greedy corporations
Aramco, Walmart, Halliburton,
go to thy damnation!

Water's getting scarce,
poison's in the skies.
City populations
are meeting their demise.

Oh, our tiny planet,
object of neglect,
Where's your angel, pure and strong,
to save us? Wait! Do I detect . . .

Some kind of newfound energy?
A child of only seven,
Facing tanks, troops and assassins,
showing another heaven . . .

Is this child the Savior
our planet sorely needs?
I don't know, but I like the thought.
Lord, please hear our pleas!

CHAPTER TEN

In the Image of God

The mountainous rainforest in Northwest Rwanda had been ignored by humans for most of its history. The terrain was too steep for even Rwandans to do their contour farming, and the climate was wet, cold, and uncomfortable most of the year. Leeches seemingly hung on every blade of grass, and the rare species of golden monkeys and 18-inch worms had never drawn much interest from scientists.

This changed in the mid-1960s when archaeologist Louis Leakey inspired and supported three young women to study primates in different areas of the world. The first—and best known, was England's Jane Goodall, who was sent to the Gombe Reserve on Lake Tanganyika to study a population of chimpanzees. The second was Holland's Birute Galdikas, who was sent to Borneo to study a population of orangutans. The third was Dian Fossey, an occupational therapist from Kentucky who was sent to the *Parc National des Virungas* in Rwanda to study a diminishing population of mountain gorillas.

Dian was the first human known to have voluntary contact with gorillas in the wild. One day a juvenile touched her hand, and soon afterward Dian was able to sit among them and play with them. She became particularly fond of a young gorilla called Digit, and was devastated in 1974 when Digit was shot and killed by poachers. Tragically, on December 26, 1985, Dian herself was found dead in her cabin, murdered by persons unknown.

It was said that poachers had been planning this for a long time, but no one was brought to trial. More tragically, in 1994 an army of Rwandan Hutus massacred more than a million Tutsi men, women and children for their race alone; and the formerly peaceful country of Rwanda became known as a land of genocide. In 1996, a Tutsi army regained control of Rwanda and began a long, painful period of reconciliation.

One of the effects of the genocide was to further endanger the gorillas of the *Parc National des Virungas*. Nearby villagers grew more and more desperate for food and farmland, and kept hacking up the mountainside of the gorilla habitat to grow more maize and soy beans. "Who is more important?" some of them argued, "Gorillas or humans? We are made in God's image, and gorillas are certainly not."

With this thought in their alcoholic minds, one night a group of five young men set forth by torchlight on a path up the mountain to where a local gorilla family was nesting. They carried high-powered rifles and talked about how many women they'd each had in the last few hours. As they approached, the gorillas lay still, hoping that the hunters would not find them in the dark. In most circumstances this would have worked, but one of the hunters had an infra-red telescopic sight attached to his gun.

Shots rang out in the night—five, seven, nine. The testicles were cut off the largest male, and the young men grabbed them, still bleeding, and tried to eat them to make themselves more potent with the village women. As they did this, they laughed at how many more women they could "get," and which ones would try, unsuccessfully, to resist. As the names of some of the village women were mentioned, the five young men broke into hysterics and rolled on the ground, they thought it was so funny.

One of the gorillas who was not shot was Gigi, a granddaughter of Digit and a being of exceptional kindness, even among the kindhearted gorilla species. She remained in her nest in the darkness, staring at her mate and two of her children, all dead in front of her. She watched the killers laughing. And, in the midst of large gorilla tears, she wondered how this could be. How could this horrible killing of her family bring her such grief and them such mirth? What was this species—humankind?

Eventually, the men noticed Gigi. They decided to stun her and bring her to men who would pay big money (perhaps $100) to buy her and send her to a zoo. A simple task for men with guns, nets, cages, and a will to make it work.

The next morning, Gigi woke up in what must have felt like Gorilla Hell. She was alone, nauseous, exhausted, and lying on the cold metal of the floor of a cage, without food, water, or her family. Some gorillas might have let out an enormous yell while cuffing their chests and beating against the bars; but Gigi was different. She was a gentle soul. She loved her family so much, and she had never meant harm to anyone. She just moaned and wept.

As men put ropes around many parts of her, Gigi did not resist. Although she had more muscles than all of the men combined, she was heartbroken and in shock. *Whatever happens, happens,* she thought. *It doesn't matter any more.*

At that point, something curious occurred, although Gigi was in no state to take notice. A little girl in a wheelchair appeared at the edge of the forest. The men, still intoxicated from drinking all night, started making jokes about her as she wheeled her way toward them. Within a minute, the men were sound asleep on the ground, the little girl had unlocked the cage, the ropes had fallen from the gorilla, and the little girl was inside the cage hugging Gigi.

There are no words in any primate language to describe the feelings which were shared by these two beings. They remained in that position for more than an hour, just feeling the tenderness, the sorrow, and the joy of each other. Then the little girl wheeled her chair outside the cage and the gorilla followed. Gigi gave the little girl one last hug and disappeared into the rainforest to find the three members of her family who had survived the attack. The little girl joined her two attendants, and they disappeared.

Stories abounded in the village and the nation about what had happened. The men swore that they had seen a little girl in a wheelchair, but these men were already in disrepute and had been intoxicated at the time. Few believed them.

More important was what happened later that day. Throughout the perimeter of the entire *Parc National de Virungas,* a strange element came into the air. Humans who had been inside the park became sick and were forced to leave. Others desiring to enter the park became sick and changed their plans. The strange air even reached the sky overhead, so that helicopters could not fly in this area. Curiously, the strange air did not affect any other species of plant or animal. The *Parc National de Virungas* became a human-free zone.

When reports of these events reached the outside world, there was little interest except by scientists and environmentalists. A few scientists were angry that they'd been deprived of their vital research and demanded a full investigation. Environmentalists were ecstatic. They wanted to find out what this new air was and use it for a thousand parks around the world.

When Rich Barton read this story, he wept, for he had met this same gorilla family on his trip two years ago. He had ventured to within five feet of them, leaning back on his haunches to reveal he was not a threat. He had looked straight into Gigi's eyes and felt a deep connection. And at that moment he had dreamed of a mysterious shield to protect the whole Virundi forest from mankind.

"Honey," Rich called to Maria, "It's happened again, this time in Rwanda." When she came to his office, he said, "The question I'm asking now is *'Why me?'* Is it because I'm a dwarf? There are thousands of dwarfs in this country alone. So why me? Is it because I've been to all these places? There are countless people who have been to more places than I have. Is it because I've had all these thoughts? There are plenty of people who are smarter than I am, and have had more thoughts than me about this world. *So why me?*

"Then, if you think about it," he continued, "this little girl hasn't done anything original. Up until now, she's just followed my imaginary plan for the planet. It's almost as if I'm in control here. And if I start imagining something she might do it for me. It's so bizarre! What do you think?"

"Sweetie," she replied, "You have so many interesting friends. Why don't you look to them for help?"

CHAPTER ELEVEN

The Prayer

The Las Vegas residence of David Plotkin, the world's greatest magician, was like no other in the world. It was set back in the mountains, hidden from everyone except aerial viewers. Surrounded by thick medieval walls with towers, and with state-of-the-art surveillance equipment, David's privacy was assured. Inside the fortress, as one might expect, there was exquisite landscaping with palm trees, waterfalls, streams and pools. There was a Sphinx similar to that at Giza, a replica of India's Taj Mahal, and a large golden object in the shape of Aladdin's mythical lamp. Cheetahs ran wild on the grounds—David's answer to the famous lions and tigers of his good friends, Siegfried and Roy.

Frequent guests included animal trainers, skilled carpenters, stage managers, pyrotechnicians, celebrities, beautiful women and many of the world's finest magicians. On special occasions, David would arrive at the drawbridge entrance with his guests, "walk" across the moat, and then pass mysteriously through the thick stone wall. When the guests arrived through the more conventional door, he and two cheetahs would lead them to Aladdin's lamp, which he would rub and watch as purple smoke rose into the air and formed the shape of a genie. The genie would bellow in a deep voice, "What is your wish, Master?"

David would reply, "A swim, please."

The genie would reply, "Yes, Master," and disappear. Then the lamp would suddenly transform itself into a magnificent jewel-studded pool. David would dive in, disappear under the water, and reappear five seconds later directly behind the group in totally dry black clothes. The group would then be directed to their quarters—suites adorned with exotic art and curiosities from different cultures. Later, they would meet for dinner at the Taj Mahal.

But at this moment David was not to be found at any of these places, nor was he on tour. He was alone, at home, in his favorite place of meditation, the Sphinx. This was a structure in the shape of a kneeling lion which had no apparent entrance or exit. Few had ever been inside, although David allowed the objects inside to be displayed occasionally at appropriate venues. The Sphinx contained the finest collection of magic memorabilia in the world, and David saw it as a spiritual connection to the past and the future.

The earliest items in the collection were three clay cups and matching balls from Mesopotamia, dating back to 1500 B.C. David smiled, thinking of how some early conjurer in robes may have used them to entertain in a town square. Another smile came as he looked at Baron Von Wolfgang's "Automaton Chess Player," which had defeated Napoleon, Ben Franklin and other notables in the late eighteenth century. Next to it was a tree of "The Father of Magic," Jean Eugene Robert-Houdin, who had used it to produce oranges at Buckingham Palace for Queen Victoria before two butterflies carried a handkerchief to her. There was a "floating head" used by the infamous Professor de Vere, an electric chair used for "self-sacrifice" by Herr Alexander, an artillery piece which fired cannonballs caught by the Great Patrizio, and much more. There was a whole room of objects used by Harry Houdini, including the Chinese water torture tank which almost took his life.

As David looked at each of these items, he thought of how relatively easy it had been to entertain audiences before the advent of motion pictures. He also thought back on his own first road shows in the late 1970s. He knew then that he needed illusions that were larger than any auditorium to return magic to the headlines. Indeed, his own section of the museum was mostly photographs, for the principal objects couldn't fit in a building like this. The seven-ton jet plane which he made disappear in 1981, the Statue of Liberty which he vanished in 1983, and the Great Wall of China which he walked through in 1986, were all part of the advancement of his profession to a new height.

David smiled again as he looked at a 1990 photograph of himself tied up and chained to a burning raft as it headed over Niagara Falls. *What a life!* he thought. *How many people get to do this kind of nonsense for a living?*

David's other 1990s photographs included him hanging in a

straitjacket ten stories above fiery spikes, flying through the air weightlessly with a lady from a Berlin audience, and being cut in two by a screeching 33-foot Death Saw. In the past ten years, he had given more than 500 shows in 100 cities around the world.

Suddenly, as if by magic, a very short man appeared at David's side, dressed in casual clothes and looking tense.

"I've been expecting you," said David.

"Good," Rich Barton answered, "I need your telepathic powers, and anything else I can find, to help me understand what's happening in my life."

"Come over here," said the greatest magician in the world. "Let me show you the latest addition to my museum." They passed under a sign reading "The Future of Magic," through a dark cave, and into a room with sparkling jewels on all sides, like the legendary mine of Snow White's seven dwarfs.

On one side of the room was a large screen. They sat down on soft chairs in front of it. David turned on a machine which projected the photograph of the little girl confronting the Israeli tanks in Jerusalem.

"Look at her body posture," said David. "She appears lifeless except for her face and hands." David read an excerpt from the corresponding article and commented, "How would it be possible to stop tanks from firing their guns—in a real setting? This is beyond magic."

Alongside this picture was placed the photograph of her in shackles at the Baghdad Interrogation Room. "Yes," David said, "this is the same child. Note the similar position of the legs, the similar tilt of her head to the left, and the dark eyebrows." The projection zoomed in on her face in the interrogation room. "Note the small mole on her neck, and the hair on her cheek. Her lips are chapped, and her black hair is rough. I don't think she has ever used shampoo or conditioner. And look at the intensity and maturity of the expression on her face. This is no ordinary child."

Rich asked, "Have you ever heard of someone doing these kind of things?"

"In history," David replied. "The closest thing I can think of are the miracles Moses reportedly performed before the pharaoh of his time. Through the Lord, Moses is said to have turned his staff into a snake, turned water into blood, and had all Egyptian first-born sons die of the plague. But that was long ago. There are no events like these in modern times."

Next, David read an excerpt from the Baghdad article. "How could she could breach that level of security to get to the Operations Room?" he asked. He added, with a smile, "That's something that only an insider—or a master illusionist like me, could do."

He read from the article about the subsequent sickness of American troops and their sudden withdrawal from Iraq. "Making thousands of soldiers sick? Now that would be difficult. Maybe something put in the water—but just the right dose, and spread it around evenly to thousands of American troops . . . with no Iraqis affected. Hmmm!"

Next he projected a photograph of the little girl being attacked by the swordsman at the sacred *Kaaba*. "Now that I could do," he said with a smile. "With some preparation and some assistance. But of course, being Jewish, I wouldn't go near the place."

David ran a video of the incident taken from one of the security cameras at the *Kaaba*. The action was frozen at the moment that the sword stopped at the little girl's neck. David said, "It looks like the sword just froze there. No bounce. As if it had met some soft, sticky, substance. But nothing like that was visible. Pretty good!"

He froze the action at the point at which the little girl broke the sword in two. "Look, she has hardly any muscles at all. I'm amazed she could lift it." David ran the sequence over and over. "I don't see how she could do this," he concluded. "There's some other force at work."

Next David read an article about the incident in Darfur, which, he said, "makes no sense, except in the pattern of things that are happening elsewhere."

Then he read about the most recent incident in the *Parc National de Virungas*. He projected an old photograph of Gigi. "What a beautiful animal your friend is!" he exclaimed. "So thoughtful, so wise, so reverent!" At this point, David's demeanor changed from one of thought to one of emotion. He began to ponder the unthinkable for a magician—that this little girl was using *real* powers, not illusions. And her object was not to entertain or earn money, but to make this a better world.

Both magicians stared at the face of Gigi—that big beautiful, spiritual face—and thought of the immense pain she must be feeling in missing her family. Somehow this became a symbol for suffering in the world—for starving children, for people dying of cancer, and for so many others who had lost hope.

David felt the suffering he knew some of his relatives had endured in the holocaust. Rich felt the suffering of his friend Dan Turner, who had recently died from AIDS.

The magicians began to cry. Then they hugged, knelt down together in this new part of the museum, and prayed.

CHAPTER TWELVE

The Peacemaker

The drive from Ghana's airport at Accra to the downtown area always struck U. N. Secretary General Kofi Annan as a sham. Tall coconut trees waving in the air, nice buildings freshly painted, no beggars, no sewers, no garbage. You might think that this was a First World country if you didn't turn onto any of the side streets, and if you didn't venture away from the hotel and conference areas.

This time the Secretary General's taxi took him directly to his office. It was nice that his plane had been delayed, and that the usual throng of welcomers had not been told the actual time of his arrival. Even the local bodyguards had gone back to bed, thinking that he wouldn't land until tomorrow.

Most of his family now lived in Geneva or New York. Many of his old friends had passed away or had been out of touch through the years. He had few ties with his old neighborhood, and yet this was his real home, the place where he'd grown up and learned about life and love, about sickness and hunger, and sbout high-life music and laughter. Some thought it was a waste of money for him to keep an apartment and an office here. He hardly ever used them. But he needed them to keep in touch with his roots, and with the challenges of people in the Third World.

He was alone as he said goodbye to the taxi driver, showed his credentials to the attendant at the front door of the office building, and went up to the third floor. An old key unlocked his office door, and he smiled. *Still works,* he thought.

The office had not changed in the two years since he'd last been there. Dust had accumulated on the desk and book shelves, but that could be easily remedied. The orange *kente*-cloth curtains had faded some, but were still a stunning piece of local culture. He played on the two large drums in the corner and noted that their sound was a little flat. The *moncala* monkey carving was as beautiful as ever. He rubbed the stomach of an Ashanti fertility doll and thanked it "for bringing me my two children." He touched the stone and wire fetish which his grandfather had given him—a relic of the old days when superstition ruled every aspect of his family's life. On the desk was a photograph of his

Swedish wife and their children. He thought about how some of his friends admired him because she was "a goddess," and others despised him because he had broken away from his people. *There is bigotry around the world,* he thought. *This much I have learned.*

On the wall facing his desk was a mantel on which he had placed his "Hall of Heroes." He loved looking at the photographs of these ten people.

The first was U.S. President Woodrow Wilson—a stern, racist intellectual with whom he had only one thing in common. Wilson had started the League of Nations and had championed the concept of a single world organization to maintain peace and blend the needs of its many citizens. The poor President had failed to have the League ratified by his own Senate; and as European divisions grew sharper, his League became an object of ridicule. It was seen as too pure, too noble, and too impractical to be effective in a Darwinian world. But without Wilson's futile efforts, there might never have been a United Nations.

The second photograph was of Franklin and Eleanor Roosevelt. Franklin, of course, with his big smile and long cigarette holder, was the one who insisted that the world try again to have some kind of planetary peace keeper. He died just two weeks before the U.N.'s formative conference at the Dumbarton Oaks mansion in Washington, D.C. Harry Truman, his successor, respected his wishes and oversaw the creation of the United Nations in San Francisco, on June 25, 1945. This time the U.S. was in the mood for such an action. The Senate approved the UN by a vote of 89 to 2, and the United States was the first nation to turn in its ratification papers.

Meanwhile it was Eleanor, the tall, ungainly, squeaky-voiced saint, who pushed the U.N. toward the most comprehensive list of rights in human history. Its Universal Declaration of Human Rights, adopted in 1948, included everyone's right to work and have protection against unemployment; the right to rest, leisure, and holidays with pay; the right to an education; the right to adequate food, clothing, housing, and medical care; and the right "to a social and international order in which the rights and freedoms set forth in this Declaration can be fully realized." The small black man thought, *If the U.N. had achieved nothing else, then this declaration, by itself, would have been worth the effort.*

The next photograph on the mantel was of Trygve Lie, a burly Norwegian. As the first U.N. Secretary General, he had been weak and deferent, often clumsy, and known for his indulgence in fine wine and cuisine. But he also managed, gradually, to assert his position among the powers in the Security Council, and to assume the role of "spokesperson for the world." In June of 1950, when North Korean troops invaded South Korea and the world braced for what appeared to be World War III, it was Trygve Lie who brought the matter to the U.N. Security Council and led, along with Harry Truman, the effort to have the United Nations use its charter to contain the aggression of Communism.

Next was the African-American, Ralph Bunche. Born to the family of an often unemployed Detroit barber, Bunche was valedictorian of his Los Angeles high school and UCLA. He won a fellowship to Harvard, and then was asked to reorganize the Political Science Department at Howard University. "But," he told friends, "living in Washington, D.C. is like serving a prison sentence. It's extremely difficult for a Negro to maintain even a semblance of human dignity."

In 1948 Bunche became the point man for the most difficult job the United Nations has ever had: negotiating between Jews and Arabs on the respective states of Israel and Palestine. On May 14, 1948, British troops withdrew from their Palestine territory, the state of Israel was founded, and a war broke out between Israel and five of its Arab neighbors. The Arabs were badly beaten, and it was U.N. envoy Ralph Bunche who brought both sides together in a peace that lasted until 1967. For this, Bunche received the Nobel Peace Prize and was offered the post of U.S. Assistant Secretary for Near Eastern, South Asian and African Affairs. He respectfully declined—the highest post ever for an African-American—and confided to friends that it was because he didn't want to live in the segregated city of Washington, D.C.

The next four people on the "Hall of Heroes" mantel were all U.N. Secretary Generals. There was Sweden's Dag Hammarskjold, who dealt with crises at the Suez Canal and in the Congo before dying in a plane crash. There was Burma's U Thant, who tried his best to resolve the Cuban Missile Crisis and the Viet Nam War, while also arranging for the first international conferences on the environment and on women's rights. There was Peru's Javier Perez de Cuellar, who dealt with Argentina's invasion of the Falkland Islands and Saddam Hussein's invasion of Kuwait, and created the Office for Emergency Operations in Africa to help with the widespread famine. And there was Egypt's Boutro Boutros-Ghali, who did his best to handle crises in Bosnia-Herzegovina, Somalia, Bosnia, Haiti and Rwanda.

Being Secretary General, the small black man thought, has got to be the best and worst job in the world. It gives you a great platform to speak out on the most important issues of the day, without ties to a particular nation or culture. And it's Hell trying to put up with all the complaints about being too weak (when the Security Council powers want to rule anyway), too insolvent (when the rich nations don't pay their dues), and too ineffective (when the 190 member nations acted mostly in their self interest).

The tenth and last person on the "Hall of Heroes" mantel brought a chuckle to the small black man. It was someone whom few would guess would make this exalted list. Someone whom he would never have voted for—and yet, this "hero" had done everything right in one of the biggest crises of the past fifty years.

It was U.S. President George Herbert Walker Bush. After Saddam Hussein conquered and terrorized Kuwait, this president immediately went to the U.N. Security Council and received its unanimous support in giving Hussein an ultimatum to withdraw his troops. When Hussein didn't, a real worldwide coalition took back Kuwait in a war that was quick, decisive, and brought minimal casualties. *Now this,* he thought, *is what the United Nations is all about.*

He continued thinking, *How strange that this man's own*

son, with almost the same name, could ignore his father's example and, in the same area of the world, do everything wrong! Blaming the U.N. commission for not finding Iraqi weapons of mass destruction, claiming proof of the existence of such weapons, and then not finding any such weapons and never offering a single apology. Rushing to war over this when he could have gathered a real coalition in another six months. Calling the United Nations "irrelevant"—well, of course! He was making it irrelevant in his attempt to bully the world, while at the same time fueling anti-American sentiment across the globe. How did such a creature ever get elected—and then re-elected? ... And it's my fate to be Secretary General at this point in time!

The small black man put his briefcase on his old desk, opened it, and took out a parcel. This, he knew, was an impulsive move—not at all the kind of thing he usually did. He was generally a calm man, cautious, logical, steady-minded. But not now. He unwrapped the parcel, brought the object inside to the small remaining space on the mantel, and put it there.

It was a photograph of the little girl in the wheelchair.

A sharp knock on the door woke the Secretary General from his reverie. Panic spread through his mind and body as he realized that he was alone and defenseless, an easy target for an assassin. There were plenty of people who would like to see him dead. He had no weapon to defend himself, not even a pocketknife or an old spear. He decided to open the door and take whatever came his way.

As he pulled the door forward and looked out, at first he saw nothing. Then he looked down and saw a diminutive figure standing alone in the dark hallway.

"My name is Rich Barton," the man said. "I interviewed you last year. There's something I need to tell you."

"Please come in," replied the Secretary General.

They sat on soft chairs, and Rich Barton continued. "First, I must apologize for this interruption of your early morning. As you may recall from our interview, I think the world of you and

I'm certainly no threat." Rich was tense. He was breathing hard, and paused to catch his breath. "Second, I need to tell you that this little girl—whose picture I see on your wall, is going to places I have been, and fulfilling dreams I had while in those places. I don't understand it. I don't even know if I like it. But it's happening. Just watch. The next place she'll go is to Mont Hoyo, in the Ituri Forest, where she will save some of my Pygmy friends there from death by local Bantus. I know, because that's where I went next on the trip I took, two years ago. Just watch."

Both men were quiet for a while. Then the Secretary General said, "Everything about this little girl is mysterious. So what are you going to do?"

"I don't know."

"Well, my friend, you are already in Africa. I would catch the next plane for the Democratic Republic of the Congo, and go to Mont Hoyo, or wherever you think she will be. Then I would try to find her and ask some questions." He added, "Please let me know what you find."

CHAPTER THIRTEEN

The Angels

In many offices and homes around the world, new maps on the wall traced the reported appearances of the little girl, with push pins at each location. One pin was in Jerusalem, one in Baghdad, one in Mecca, one in Darfur, one in Northeastern Uganda, and one in Northwestern Rwanda.

There appeared to be a pattern in the travel of the little girl and her companions. People discussed—and even bet on, the next likely place where she would show up. Since she seemed to be heading southwest in Africa, there was some speculation that she might appear in the Congo (where neighboring tribes were still at war), in Zimbabwe (where a dictator was making life miserable for almost everyone), or maybe in another animal preserve.

Journalists, and their cousin-like paparazzi, were risking their savings to go to the areas where they figured she would arrive next, hoping to get the scoop of the day. Major newspapers and TV news networks sent their crews to places they thought she might go.

There were many discussions about who she was and what her mission might be. She evidently wanted to stop wars and to help people and animals in need. She turned up in places where there was a crisis, handled each situation in a different way, and left with no trace. She had saved many lives, and the only people she had killed were Janjaweed warriors. Even these had simply disappeared—and, who knew, they might eventually turn up somewhere.

The little girl could barely talk, and yet she didn't need to say much. She had cured millions of people from the horrific AIDS virus, but had no apparent interest in diseases like cancer and malaria. She traveled with an adoptive mother and a man, both of whose backgrounds were unknown.

The little girl's powers were a subject of debate. She never actually did anything to demonstrate that she was the one who dismantled the Israeli tanks or caused the sickness of American troops in Iraq. Nobody saw her do anything to the air at the boundaries of the rainforest in the Parc National des Virungas.

She didn't provide an anti-AIDS vaccine that was distributed to those infected through pills or injections. Things just happened, and their timing was exquisite.

The little girl had been nominated for several Nobel prizes— for Peace, Medicine and even Physics. The respective committees rejected all three nominations, saying that they needed more background information and more proof that she had done these things. "Besides," said one committeeperson, "how could we inform her of her prize if we don't know her name, her address, or how she can be reached? She doesn't even have a cell phone!"

Meanwhile, the merchant at her former home in Jerusalem had turned the house into a shrine, for which there was now a hefty admission charge for visitors. He figured that if she and Maya ever returned, he'd gladly give them back their room.

It's curious that the U.S. President temporarily lost interest in the little girl. The farther she ventured into Africa, the less he thought about her, although he did ask the Director of his new intelligence agency to "keep an eye on her." As he saw it, the little girl had done little to endanger American security, and her activities in Iraq had given him a big boost in the American polls.

The Pygmies of the Democratic Republic of the Congo and adjacent countries were a vanishing breed. Persecuted for centuries by the Bantu tribes around them, they had to live deep in the forest to escape murder, slavery and the burning of their thatched homes. Some of their ancient culture was still intact— living off of the jungle, hunting with blowguns and poisoned arrows, and laughing by cupping their armpits and rolling on the ground. They still had double marriages, in which one man and one woman of a community had to marry their counterparts from a neighboring community. But they had lost their original language, and now only spoke the language of the tribe closest to them. Many had been forced to live in barrack-like houses close to the road, with death being the penalty for returning to the jungle. They were an inherently happy people, but had suffered much under the rule of the Bantus.

Two years ago, when Rich Barton first ventured into the Ituri forest to meet the Pygmies, they greeted him like a king. He was their size and therefore "one of them," yet he also bore the confidence and wisdom of the outside world. He knew their language, Swahili. He dazzled them with his bright orange tent, and with the instant blue flame in his butane stove. When he performed just a few of his magic tricks—the vanishing cane, the fountain of silks, and the old stick and string—they came to see him as a god. He, in turn, came to see them as angels—naive, childlike and vulnerable in an often cruel world.

The Pygmy whom Rich Barton felt closest to was a slender man with sunken eyes, called Asumbo. One night they sat on a log before a small fire, and Rich tried to explain where he came from. "You get in a *piroque* (canoe)," Rich said, "and you paddle down a big river for about two moons. Then you cross a very large lake for another five moons, and then you walk on the land for another five or six moons, until you come to my home—a big house. There are no elephants there, and no monkeys or big snakes. But there are some antelope and a few lions, and lots of houses and roads. The air isn't too good, and it gets cold. But I think you'd enjoy meeting my wife and child." Rich pulled out pictures of his family, and Asumbo looked at them with great interest.

As time passed, Rich Barton found himself ill-equipped to handle life in the rainforest. Some of the Pygmies began to laugh at his frustration with things like mosquitoes, fried snakes, and their incessant chattering all night long. Then his brother Marc came to visit him and told him that their mother was gravely ill. It was time to leave.

On his last day with them, Rich heard the guns of Bantu tribesmen coming to kill his Pygmy friends for deserting their roadside homes. Rich's parting words to Asumbo were that he "would return some day soon" to help Asumbo's people.

It didn't take Rich Barton long to take a plane to Kinshasa, and then to Kisangani, gateway to the Ituri Forest. He knew that the next step—traveling across the rainforest to Mont Hoyo, the home of his Pygmy friends—would normally take days, maybe weeks, by road, but he didn't have time. He needed to arrive before the little girl did, or it would all be wasted.

In a sudden moment of craziness, he devised a plan which was extremely dangerous. He would later call it "the stupidest thing I ever did." He chartered a plane to fly over the Ituri Forest toward Mont Hoyo, and brought with him the pilot's World War II parachute, which had never been used.

As the plane flew over the dense jungle in the mid-afternoon sun, Rich had second and third and fourth thoughts about what he was doing. Yes, it was true that he had never before jumped with a parachute; but how difficult could it be? He'd seen movies—all you did was put on the parachute, jump, and then pull the rip cord. Gravity did the rest. But then again the jungle below was solid with trees, with no ground in sight. *Not to worry,* he thought. *I'll just head toward the big waterfall, where there must be a clearing somewhere.*

As the waterfall came into view, Rich thought of his wife and son at home, who would miss him terribly if something went wrong. Was this risk fair to them? Was it worth it? Then he thought of the little girl in the wheelchair, and how she was changing the world.

Yes! He needed to do absolutely everything in his power to understand her mission, and maybe help her. *Besides,* he thought, *she would never let anything bad happen to me. I'm too important to her!*

That was his final thought as Rich Barton looked at the Congolese pilot once more, watched the pilot flash him an ear-splitting grin, and then hurled his small body out the open door and into space.

The ride down went well for a while. He experienced a quixotic sense of weightlessness, and then opened his eyes. The ground was moving toward him at an alarming rate, and he yanked the rip cord. When the chute caught the air, the force on his shoulders was so strong that he almost lost consciousness, but he didn't. Then he floated, slowly, remarkably slowly, downward. When he opened his eyes again, he saw that there was no waterfall anywhere in sight, nor was there a clearing. Just big trees.

As he approached the jungle he would have braced himself for the landing had he known how to do it, but he didn't. He just let nature take its course. Within two seconds his legs crashed against something hard, his knees banged against his chin, his right arm was badly scratched, and his buttocks jerked hard against some kind of vine. Then all was calm, and he was still alive. He had survived!

Opening his eyes, he realized that he was still hanging in his chute, which had caught in the upper part of a tree. When he looked down, he could see the ground, about seventy feet below.

For the first time, he realized the seriousness of his predicament. There was no way he could climb thirty feet to the treetop. Even if he managed to do this, how then could he possibly get down? There was no way to descend seventy feet to the ground without falling and killing himself, and no tree within twenty feet on any side. Besides, he was quite entangled in the ropes of his chute. He could hang there in relative calm, with all his bruises, for a long time. But otherwise he was helpless.

Idiot! he thought. *I'm a total idiot!*

Sounds of the forest could be heard now. The "caw caw" of a bird above him, a monkey swinging in a nearby tree, and crickets.

Crickets! he thought. *That's right. It'll be getting dark soon. Boy, what an idiot I am!*

He tried practicing a little Buddhism: *Aaah so, here I am hanging from a tree, and the world out there is beautiful. I am truly one with nature, blessed to be one of the many creatures of God. And all is well . . .*

A mosquito landed on his nose. "Good grief!" he yelled as he tried to brush it off by jerking his head to the right. It stayed on his nose. He struggled to move his nose up to one of the parachute cords, and the mosquito flew away. He knew it would be back soon, with friends.

Rich envisioned a variety of jungle creatures eating him alive, bite by bite, minute by minute, over the next few days. Mosquitos, ants, snakes, buzzards, beetles, lice, and then maggots. *Was this his final mission in life—to provide a feast for critters, mostly small? How stupid he was!* He imagined what his skeleton would look like, stripped of flesh.

He thought again of Maria and Peter in their Oregon home. *Of course they would come to save him if they had any inkling of how to do it. But there was no one who knew where he was. Only that grinning pilot.*

Rich Barton might have died in that tree had he not remembered how his Pygmy friends communicated in the jungle. He yelled, "OO-EE-AY-AAY-OO-OO-UU-EE-AAY! OO-EE-AY-AAY-OO-OO-UU-EE-AAY!" He did this three times, and then waited. Then he heard the most beautiful sound imaginable—an echo of his own sound from far away. He repeated his call, and the echo came closer and closer. At last, several Pygmies appeared on the ground beneath him. Some of them recognized him, and cupped their hands against their armpits and rolled on the ground in laughter.

"Asumbo, my old buddy," Rich shouted in Swahili. "Get me out of here!"

Using long, strong vines and an impressive tree-climbing technique, the Pygmies lowered Rich to *terra firma*, which he kissed. He grabbed each of his friends in turn and gave them bear hugs while they laughed and laughed at the antics of their old friend.

He went with them to their current camp and started to describe the little girl. Less than a minute into the story, he fell asleep, exhausted from the events of the day.

Rich soon found that things had changed in the Ituri Forest since he had last been there. The Pygmies led him to their newly-painted five-bedroom treehouse with a corrugated roof, running water and an indoor toilet. They started a generator, pulled out cold cans of Coca Cola from a refrigerator, and turned on a television set. Then they proudly told him about their blow-gun exhibition tomorrow for local Bantus and some European tourists.

Rich soon realized that these Pygmies were no longer threatened in their lifestyle. Once again it was time to leave. As Rich climbed on top of a beer truck to take him to an airport and then back to his Oregon home, he once again pondered his fate in life.

Was he totally crazy, or just a little crazy? Was there anything real to the thought that he had some kind of relationship to the little girl? Was she real? Were Maria and Peter real? Was life real, or did Plato have it right? Life was just some kind of shadow on a cave wall.

CHAPTER FOURTEEN

Armageddon

Meanwhile, the little girl surprised everyone. She turned up in a place no one could possibly have foreseen.

In the old days, when security was tight in the Soviet Union, such an event could never have occurred. In those days, every Timex watch, every hearing aid, and every belt buckle on every precious pair of blue jeans was carefully examined for potential dangers to the State. Every movement of each visitor was carefully watched by the KGB, for everyone was suspected of being a spy or of fomenting treason in some form.

The highest level of security had always been maintained at the Kremlin. There were always large crowds of Russians and foreigners on the cobblestones of Red Square. Tourists came to see Lenin's tomb (the most viewed body in history) and St. Basil's Cathedral (with its beautiful onion-shaped domes hiding the cruelty of its original patron, Ivan the Terrible). The other big attraction on Red Square was Gum's, the largest retail store in Russia and a symbol of capitalism even in the days of the Communist empire.

At one side of Red Square was the Kremlin itself, a fortress enclosed by two miles of stone walls and twenty towers, built in the 12th century to keep out Mongol invaders. After the dissolution of the Communist regime in 1991, the Russian government still held its meetings there. The people of this land loved history, and the Kremlin had been their greatest symbol for close to a thousand years.

But on this day, the drama took place, not near the popular structures, but in a lower basement deep in the bowels of the Kremlin's legislative branch, the *Duma*. A container had arrived by ship on the Moscow River, and had been unloaded without inspection. Its markings indicated that it was a copy machine ordered for one of the administrative offices of the Agriculture Department. It was a heavy item in a crate five feet by three feet, by four feet tall. No one questioned its authenticity.

When it reached the proper room, the crate was dismantled and thrown away as garbage. The item inside looked like a copy machine. There was no reason to suspect it might be anything else, as countless other such items arrived daily from various places.

It took five members of the agriculture department ten minutes to move it into its proper place, and then came the magic moment. They were ready to plug it in to a 220-volt wall socket. Everyone was smiling.

They didn't know that this "copy machine" was actually an atomic bomb which, when triggered by inserting the plug in the wall socket, would have blown up the Kremlin, Moscow, and much of the surrounding area.

But just before the plug was inserted, a little girl in a wheelchair appeared in the doorway.

She said one word in Russian, "*Nyet.*"

There were angry shouts at her intrusion and at her disruption of the debut of the new machine. She continued to sit in her wheelchair amidst the commotion. Finally one of the men, just to make sure, opened the back cover and found strange wiring inside. The Kremlin bomb squad was called, the machine was carefully hauled away, and Moscow was saved. In the old days, something like this could be kept secret.

In the old days, information leakers were generally shot on the spot or sent to a Siberian *gulag*. But these were modern times. The witnesses blurted out every detail they remembered, and the story was featured in the next day's headlines. Everything was confirmed except for the presence of the little girl in the wheelchair, who had disappeared.

By itself, this might have been a forgettable episode in the annals of a bumbling nation in decline. But what followed was new, monumental and planet-transforming. It also captured the attention of the U.S. President.

Later that day, every nuclear weapon in the world—including those in Russia, China, India, Pakistan, Israel, France, England, North Korea, Saudi Arabia, South Africa, the United States, and everywhere else, was rendered unusable.

Back at his Oregon home, recovering from his many bruises,

Rich Barton puzzled over the new direction of the little girl. Yes, he had visited the Kremlin on a trip last year. He'd walked into a room where a new copier was being installed, and winced as it was being plugged into the wall, thinking that it might be a nuclear bomb. And yes, at that moment he had wished that all the world's nuclear weapons would simply become dysfunctional. This was just last year.

Now he had to ponder a new chain of events. Why? Was she playing games with him? How could she have known that the Pygmies were no longer in trouble, but Moscow was in immediate danger? Were these cross-patterns of his life with hers just coincidental?

Did she even know that he existed?

CHAPTER FIFTEEN

Righteousness

When the news broke about how the little girl had saved the city of Moscow from nuclear holocaust, she became an instant worldwide heroine. Later, when accounts came in about how the nuclear weapons of the world were no longer functional, there was deep mistrust on the part of many world leaders.

Was this "little thing" planning to take over the planet?

In view of what she had already done, she might have the power. But what was her true mission? Some leaders of nations that had nuclear weapons began to rethink their posture in the world.

Did Pakistan need to expand its ground forces to meet a conventional attack from India?

Did North Korea need to join the world community in order to procure the food its people so desperately needed?

How did such deprivation affect the two largest nuclear weapon holders, Russia and the United States?

The Secretary General tried to call an urgent meeting of the U.N. Security Council, but none of its members were ready for this. Their first concern was to look after their own nations, for the recent change had brought a shift in the balance of power.

The first thing the U.S. President did was to order a nuclear test on his "favorite" island in the South Pacific. When the bomb failed to detonate, he called an immediate cabinet meeting in the War Room, in a bunker three stories beneath the Oval office. "Gentlemen," he said, forgetting the female Secretary of State on his left, "to put it simple, America has been attacked by a foreign power, and I think it's time for a Declaration of War."

"Yes, Mr. President," said the Vice President.

"Yes, Mr. President," said the Secretary of Defense.

"Yes, Mr. President," said the new Director of Intelligence.

"Um, Mr. President," said the Secretary of Transportation, "who exactly would we declare war against, and how would we wage such a war?"

"Well it's clear that a foreign power has decapacitated our nucular defense system. Just like with Al Qaeda, we need to destroy that power—whatever it takes."

"But," the Secretary of Transportation continued, "all we know is that a little girl was seen in the vicinity of a Russian bomb, and that she may have kept it from exploding."

"That's enough for me," said the President. "Do you think we can afford to wait until she attacks us directly, like with 9-11? Hell no! I'm not taking any chances with the lives of so many Americans at stake! I want her shot, dead, incinerated—whatever it takes!"

"But," said the Secretary of Transportation amid scowls from others in the room, "much of the world sees her as a saint. After all she did save Moscow, and she mostly tries to help people."

"Look," said the President impatiently, while thinking about the need to fire this lone dissenter, "how about . . . we don't say anything about this, Okay? We just kill her and pretend it was an accident. Okay?"

"Sounds good to me," said the Secretary of Defense. "We've got the finest death squads in the world, if I may say so."

"I like it," said the Secretary of State. "It's simple, it's bold, and it's American. It's the kind of thing we've stood for throughout our history. It's what makes us great!"

"Hail to the Chief!" said the Secretary of the Army.

After they all said "Hail!", the President beamed with pride and said, "I guess we've done our work, fellas. This meeting is adjourneyed."

And so it was that American death squads went to all corners of the world looking for the little girl, as if she could be easily found. Sightings of little girls in wheelchairs with various ailments came in from a thousand places, and were checked out to no avail. A number of little girls came close to being blown to bits by overzealous death squads, and the Secretary of State had to intervene to smooth ruffled feathers.

Meanwhile, publicly, the U. S. President proclaimed with a confident smile, "Our nucular weapons system is as strong as ever—never better!"

*****

"'Never better,'" Rich Barton muttered to the television set in his office. "As if we believe anything you say!"

"What, dear?" Maria answered from the kitchen. "Is something wrong?"

"Everything's wrong," Rich replied. "I just can't seem to figure out who I am these days, or what's happening to me."

"Dad," said young Peter, at his side, "can I help? Do you want a hug?"

"Yes."

CHAPTER SIXTEEN

The Pentecost

Mike McKleroy was one of Rich Barton's long-time friends. Mike had grown up with all the graces—St. George's Academy, Yale, Hastings Law School. But then he veered a little to the left—hunting for treasure with real pirates off the coast of Honduras, leading expeditions on searches for Bigfoot in the Trinity Alps, and having his own close encounter with "the Grays—a species with black, almond-shaped eyes from the Zeta Reticuli star system, who have been collecting eggs and sperm from Earthlings for years as part of their interbreeding program."

Rich maintained a healthy skepticism toward Mike's accounts until recently, when nothing else appeared to explain the activities of the little girl.

My God! Rich thought, in a breakthrough moment. *Maybe Mike has been right all along!*

Rich called Mike and asked whether there were any flying saucer conventions going on.

"Rich," Mike answered with a scornful tone, "We don't say 'flying saucers' any more. We call them UFOs—Unidentified Flying Objects, and people who study them are called 'Ufologists.'"

"Sorry, Mike," said Rich. "Are their any ufologist conventions coming up?"

"You bet," answered Mike. "There's a big one this weekend in Roswell, New Mexico. I wouldn't miss it for the galaxy."

The conversation continued, with lots of questions about what goes on at these things, and about proper attire. "Well," said Mike, "normally you find all kinds of people there. Some of them, surprisingly, are dressed in suits and ties and are reputable scientists and businessmen."

Rich thought, *I can believe the businessmen, but scientists?*

"Then," Mike continued, "you have others who are, well, I guess you could say a little weird. A lot of them dress up like Captain Kirk, or Spock, or Obi-wan Kinobe, or R2-D2, or the group in the Star Wars bar scene. Some are just doing it for fun, but others actually believe they are these creatures. You can't really have a normal conversation with them, and you'd better be careful. Now this time—I almost forgot, it's a special convention to honor the latest alien, so everyone will be arriving in wheelchairs.'

"Wheelchairs?" said Rich. "Does that mean that we have to rent wheelchairs to get in?"

"Well," Mike replied, "I don't think so. There's an area-wide shortage of wheelchairs, due to the convention, so I don't think anyone could get them at this late date."

The two old friends met at Mike's house, left their car at the Oakland Airport, and flew off to Roswell. After a stop in Los Angeles, they landed at the airport in Albuquerque and rented a car to take them the rest of the way.

It was the most beautiful drive Rich had taken in a long time. Pushing out of the red desert were candelabra cacti, pinion pines and large mesas. In the distance was snow-covered Carrizo Peak, a holy mountain to local Indians.

Rich and Mike arrived at the small town of Roswell at sunset. It might have been any other town in the southwest, except for the sign directing visitors to the International UFO Museum. Rich and Mike were lucky to find the last available room at Mission Mars, where they settled in for a good night's sleep.

The sun was shining the next morning as the two travelers walked across the street to the Cup and Saucer Café. On the walls were photographs of flying saucers through the years. They settled into a booth beneath a signed photograph of Robin Williams from his Mork and Mindy days. Rich ordered Plutocakes and Orion Juice, while Mike had an Omegalette with a Sagittarius sweet roll on the side.

"Say," Mike whispered to Rich, "I think that's Dr. Barbara Blake in the corner. She's famous for her work with the SETI Project." Rich, the ever-curious dwarf, walked over to the silver-haired woman in a dark blue pants suit, introduced himself, and asked her to join them for breakfast. Saying she "could use some company," she came over and sat down opposite them in the booth.

"I've heard of your good work with SETI," said Mike. "Maybe you could tell Rich about it."

"Well," she said, "SETI stands for Search for Extraterrestrial Intelligence. It's a scientific organization started in 1960 and funded by NASA, which is trying to receive signals from beings in outer space. You see, we're almost positive that there are other advanced forms of life out there. With one hundred billion stars in our Milky Way galaxy, and at least fifty to one hundred billion other galaxies like ours that we know of, the chances are overwhelming that we are not alone in the universe. We've been sending radio signals to outer space for the last eighty years, but we have yet to hear from them. Won't it be exciting to hear from an alien in space for the first time?"

"Have you heard anything at all so far?" Rich asked.

"No, but if we don't open our ears through the SETI program, we're certain to hear nothing."

"What do you think of the other UFO people who will be attending this convention?"

"Well," Dr. Blake sighed, "I can tell you they don't like us. They think we're wasting our time looking deep into space when they think they've already found aliens here on Earth. But we're scientists who need more than unverifiable eyewitness accounts to make conclusions about something so important."

"What do you think about the little girl in the wheelchair?" Mike asked.

"That's a good case in point," she replied. "So far, we have no scientific evidence to suggest that she's done anything unusual, in spite of the strange occurrences around her. And yet these people here at the convention—you'll meet them—they worship her like a god."

The convention site was a large flat sandy area on a private ranch, only five miles from the spot where an alien spacecraft was reputed to have crashed on July 8, 1947. Most of the people in attendance were dressed casually in jeans and sweaters, but a great many came in motorized wheelchairs. There were a few who came dressed as space monsters of various sorts—green Martians with horns and tails, bug-like creatures with antennae and scales, and a one-eyed squid with 8-foot long tentacles gathering dust behind her. There were also some who hadn't had time to buy or make costumes, so they resorted to what they had—a Mickey Mouse outfit, a Bart Simpson suit, a torn Sponge Bob, and a ragged Easter Bunny. It was all in good fun, with a potential for the serious side.

The program went mostly according to plan. The first day was reserved for "traditional" paranormal presentations. Colin Andrews, "the world's foremost authority on crop circles," stated that while 80% of these were clearly manmade, a full 20% of them were unexplained. Dr. Roger Leir spoke about the difficulties of alien implant removal, and there was a special presentation by Earlene and Shurlene, two women who claimed to have been abducted by space aliens.

The second day was devoted to "eyewitnesses" of the little girl in the wheelchair. These were people who claimed not only to have seen her, but to have visited her spaceship and her planet in another galaxy. The energy of the crowd grew stronger as time passed, as preparations were made for the final event, called the "Run for the Sun."

There are many versions of what actually happened that night, but there are also a few points on which all could agree. Half a mile from the stage, a pile of logs in the shape of an enormous ball had been constructed to look like the sun, and all around it was an asphalt track as wide as a football field. The concept was that "the sun" would be set on fire, producing prodigious heat and light, and at some point everyone in wheelchairs would start moving around it counterclockwise. They would go around "the sun" faster and faster and faster and faster, until at last they exceeded the speed of light, at which point the little girl would realize that some people on Planet Earth had reached her planet's advanced level of technology, and would appear in her wheelchair in the center of the sun and lead them to her planet, where, as Mike put it, she and other similar life forms "would feel free to study us, breed with us, and do anything they pleased with us."

It was a slight variation of the 1917 test of Einstein's Specific Theory of Relativity, which had measured perturbations in the speed of light as it passed by Mercury and the Sun.

At the stroke of midnight, someone used a torch to light "the sun," which had so much gasoline on it that it nearly exploded like a bomb.

From where Rich and Mike stood, they were sure that some people had gotten burned.

Nevertheless, the ritual continued, with "the sun" getting ever hotter and brighter and the wheelchair participants lined up behind each other, revving their engines like drivers at the Indy 500. At some point, a man who looked like an obese Rasputin waved a checkered flag and ran as fast as he could to get out of the way of the wheelchair mob. There was such shouting by the drivers and onlookers alike that the normally serene New Mexico desert exploded with human noise, which eventually turned into a chant:

> *Run for the sun, Run for the sun,*
> *Faster than the speed of light And then we've won!*
>
> *Run for the sun! Run for the sun!*
> *Faster than the speed of light And then we've won!*
>
> *RUN FOR THE SUN! RUN FOR THE SUN!*
> *FASTER THAN THE SPEED OF LIGHT AND THEN*
> *WE'VE WON!*
>
> *RUN FOR THE SUN! RUN FOR THE SUN!*
> *FASTER THAN THE SPEED OF LIGHT AND THE*
> *WE'VE WON!*

Rich and Mike stood there, amazed, watching the large group of wheelchair riders, many of them in strange costumes, zooming around this enormous ball of fire and chanting their mantra in unison at the top of their lungs, while trying to make their vehicles go faster than the speed of light. The slower wheelchairs tended to stay near the center, while the really fast ones circled the outside at a breakneck pace.

Rich was sure that he heard a couple of jet engines among the group, and some of the speeds were far, far faster than any wheelchair he'd ever seen.

Suddenly someone shouted, "There she is!" and everyone looked toward "the sun."

"The Little Girl!" someone screamed. Then came cries like, "Wow!", "I don't believe it!" and "No way!"

"What do you see?" Rich asked Mike.

"I see a little girl in a wheelchair," said Mike, "sitting in the center of the fire."

"You *do?*" exclaimed Rich. "I'm looking there as hard as I can, and I don't see anything but flames!"

"Well," said a young girl in a pink flamingo costume standing near Rich, "Do you believe in aliens?"

"Umm," replied Rich. "I don't really know."

"Well then," said the young girl, "that explains it. How can you see God if you're not a believer?"

CHAPTER SEVENTEEN

A Cloud Over the Earth

F or thousands of years, China had been considered by its residents to be the center of the world. The Chinese people were particularly proud of its many dynasties, its Great Wall, its invention of products like paper and gunpowder, and the sheer enormity of its geography and population.

Normally, visitors to Beijing stayed at one of the large international hotels and took tourist buses to Tiananmen Square, to the palace of the last Emperor, and to a small section of the Great Wall. But the little girl and her entourage were anything but normal. Their sudden and totally unexpected appearance was at the door of one of the pulmonary wards of the Beijing People's Hospital. The scene was busy—too few doctors and nurses for the many patients, and noisy with the shouts, coughs, and wheezes of people struggling to breathe.

As a security guard asked the visitors for their credentials, the little girl in the wheelchair leaned toward one of the patients, a middle-aged woman who had worked in a nearby coal-fired power station. The worker was gasping for air, thinking back over her proud life of service to the state, and wishing she were dead. The little girl looked deep into the woman's eyes. There was a union of spirits, a natural reaching out of arms toward each other, a sweet embrace, and tears.

They stayed that way for a long time, despite the attempts of security guards to get the attention of the little girl. The rest of the story is murky. The little girl and her companions left. The woman miraculously got better and returned to her home. And all carbon-powered traffic in Beijing came to a halt.

At first it seemed like a joke. Many in Beijing laughed at the predicament of others, until they realized that they, too, would have to walk miles to work and home—or take electric public transportation, or ride their old bicycles, which had been sitting in storage.

Then the leader of China declared this to be something like an act of war, and he blamed the U.S. and its President. There was an exchange of harsh words, and internal political points were scored as both the Chinese and American leaders rallied their citizenry to arm against the respective enemies. But then China backed off from this stance and instituted major anti-pollution reforms, which they said they'd been planning all along.

Meanwhile, at exactly the same moment that the little girl and her two followers appeared in the hospital in Beijing, an identical threesome was reportedly seen at the door of a pulmonary ward of the National Hospital of Workers in Bangkok, Thailand. The little girl leaned over a middle-aged man suffering from a terminal lung disorder, hugged him for a long time, and left. The man miraculously recovered and went home.

And, as in Beijing, that same day all carbon-powered traffic in the greater Bangkok area came to a halt. There was laughter, consternation, and then cries of terrorism by the central government. Bangkok citizens had to immediately change their plans in order to get to work and back, and to do other chores in their normal day. But, over time, the leaders and the people of Thailand adjusted by making Bangkok a carbon-free city.

The economic cost of these two alterations in major cities was vast. People working in the carbon-based transportation sector lost their jobs, although many were soon re-employed in the emergency effort to produce more electric vehicles and bicycles.

Stock markets around the world adjusted with declines in oil stocks and rises in the stocks of electric car manufacturers. Those in charge of security puzzled over how they might have taken precautions to avert such a disaster. And people everywhere scratched their heads over what was happening to the world.

Back on the porch of his Oregon home, Rich Barton scratched his head too, partly to deal with those Congo mosquito bites. "Honey," he said to Maria, "I was in both of those pulmonary wards—the one in Beijing, and later the other in Bangkok. Of course I didn't visit them *simultaneously*—the little show-off!"

"Daddy," said Peter, "why didn't the little girl meet with you in the jungle? Does that mean she doesn't like you?"

Rich pondered this question and then answered, "Sweetie, this little girl does everything I want her to do. So she's got to like me. Get it? But maybe she's a little shy. After all, I'm a pretty powerful person and she's probably just waiting for the right time."

A skeptical Peter wrinkled his brow.

"So where's she going next?" asked Maria.

"New Delhi," answered Rich. "But this time I'm staying here. I'm not so good with burning brides."

CHAPTER EIGHTEEN

The Goddess of Destruction

"**G**od dammit, I told you guys to find her and kill her, and that's my number one priority around here! What the hell's going on?" The President of the United States, back in the War Room in rolled-up shirt sleeves, was shouting at his joint chiefs of staff and cabinet members.

"Mr. President," replied the Secretary of Defense, "we're doing all we can, but she's slippery. She doesn't seem to hang out the way other people do. She doesn't really have a home, and she kind of drifts around the world."

"Mr. President," said the Secretary of State in a tone designed to soften the mood. "I like the way you handled the Chinese premier. Very *adroit.*"

The President beamed as he thought, *Never heard that word before, but I think it means something good.*

"Mr. President," said the Chairman of the Joint Chiefs of Staff, "Our death squads are on high alert. We won't give up 'til we get her, I promise."

"Mr. President," said the Secretary of Transportation, "I'm thinking we might want a contingency plan, just in case she stops the carbon-powered vehicles around here. How about setting up an emergency system in which non-carbon vehicles are on the ready to bring important people to where they need to go? We might also expand the capacity of our light-rail system in the big cities."

"What?" the President bellowed, "and be laughed out of town by my oil buddies—saying a little girl is now setting policy in the great U.S. of A? No way! I won't consider it. Besides, the transition would cost all kinds of jobs, and my stocks—I mean the oil stocks, would go into free fall."

"Mr. President," the new EPA Director said cautiously, "making some move in this direction would help the environmental vote, even if it was just a speech."

"You're ignoring my base," the President replied angrily. "Never forget who got us here—big oil, big defense contractors, big pharmaceuticals, big money, and God-fearing Americans. I'll never let them down!"

"Mr. President," said the U.N. Ambassador, "other nations on the Security Council are proposing a resolution to support the little girl and her activities. How should we react to this?"

The President looked at the Ambassador in silence for a few moments. Then, as if a light bulb went on in his brain, he said, "In times of crisis, we must be bold. We can't let the U.N. or any other hostile power stand in the way of American security. I want you to pre-empt them. Propose a coalition of war against the little girl and her followers—we'll call them a nation, and use all our influence to get as many votes as possible. You know, threats to cut off military aid, medicine, food, tents, wooden legs—stuff like that. And for the East Europeans, remind them that it was the U.S. of A. that got rid of their godless communist dictators. Tell everyone that if they don't vote with us on this, they're un-American. You know what I mean. Use my motto: 'If you're not with us, you're with the terrorists!'"

"Yes, Mr. President," said the entire cabinet in unison.

Cities in other nations around the world were not so resistant to change. Indeed, the use of light rail commuter trains was expanded in Berlin, Mexico City, Sao Paulo, Shanghai, and Tokyo, and there was talk about "carbon-free zones" in many parts of the world. Beijing reviewed the state of emission controls on its coal plants, and the nation tightened its standards on auto emissions. It even erected a statue to the little girl in Tiananmen Square.

Other cities in the little girl's projected path, like Manila and Djakarta, anticipated her arrival and started improving not only the air quality but the water quality of local rivers. They removed graffiti and garbage from the streets. Most of the people in these places saw the little girl as a positive figure, and even hung signs of welcome in the local hospitals just in case she dropped in.

But the little girl and her two companions changed direction again. This time they headed west, to India's capital of New Delhi. In the kitchen of a luxurious private home near the Rajpath, New Delhi's broadest avenue and the scene of a pageant every year on Republic Day, a beautiful young bride trembled in terror. The family of her new husband had demanded more dowry payment from her family, and her family was unable to pay. The bride's mother-in-law and new aunt had just poured a cup of gasoline over her head and the aunt had just lit a match and was ready to burn the poor girl to death.

"Please don't do it!" the young bride screamed. "I'll do anything! *Please, don't kill me!!*"

The aunt ignored the pleas and was ready to throw the lit match at the bride when suddenly three people appeared: the young girl in the wheelchair, accompanied by Maya and Joseph. In spite of their appearance, the aunt would have thrown the match had she not witnessed an even more terrifying sight. The little girl's body transformed itself into Durga, the Goddess of Destruction, with a thousand arms waving a thousand swords at the aunt.

The aunt had the presence of mind to blow out the match before fainting on the kitchen floor. The mother-in-law ran screaming from the scene. As devout Hindus, they got the message.

The message was also received in other parts of India's Hindu community, particularly as more Durgas appeared in similar circumstances in other kitchens throughout the country. And so the practice of bride-burning was suddenly ended, after many centuries—millennia, of cruelty and suffering.

In Delhi, as in Beijing, a statue of the little girl in the wheelchair was erected, this one near a monument to Gandhi, and people came there to worship and reflect on her teachings.

On their back porch, Peter Barton was playing miniature cars with his friends Dillon and Miranda. "Daddy," he said, "where are the little girl and her friends going next? Are they coming here to visit us?"

"Not yet," Rich replied. "I think they might go to Indonesia. And I think I'll stay here this time, too. She probably doesn't need my help."

Maria rolled her eyes and shook her head with a grin.

CHAPTER NINETEEN

The Good Earth

S ome people noted a pattern in the little girl's behavior. She made appearances at the center of a social problem, fixed that problem, and went on to do something more sweeping in terms of a larger solution. But she was also known for surprises—nobody had expected her to go from Rwanda to Moscow, or to show up simultaneously in Beijing and Bangkok.

She broke the pattern once again when she manifested three changes around the world without actually showing up anywhere at all. Of course, no one could be sure she was behind these changes. There was no evidence that she was the "perpetrator," and yet nothing else could explain the strange events, or their timing.

The first occurred deep in the cavities of the earth. It was detected by a lone British geologist, who had been contracted by Saudi Arabia to go to the oasis of Wadi Falla and remeasure the dimensions of the planet's largest oil reserve. Using an advanced technique involving five-mile deep explosions and surface seismographs, he was trying to measure the exact parameters of the field's oil and natural gas deposits. He conducted these tests, but was unable to detect any petrochemicals at all. He carefully re-examined the data, brought in a consultant (who was no help), and then detonated a second charge to produce another set of data. For this second test, he even used two sets of instruments—just in case one was faulty.

But the oil field was still missing.

He called in other consultants, who were equally puzzled by the change. After all, large oil fields don't just suddenly disappear. Their *modus operandi* is to just sit there, unchanged, for million of years, until somebody came along to remove the oil.

More problematic was the question of what to do about this. The Saudi Oil Minister himself had contracted the geologist for the job, and the Minister would no doubt report such "negligence" to the King himself. The poor geologist would be fired and his reputation forever besmirched. So, rather than go to the minister and advise him of the problem, the geologist simply submitted a report without conclusions or recommendations and hoped that the Minister wouldn't notice. Maybe the geologist would get lucky, and some other poor contractor would get stuck with the mess, or maybe there was no mess at all—just faulty instruments or whatever, and his life would go on as it had before.

That didn't happen. The Saudi Minister noticed the absence of the oil field in the report right away and, without further consultation or anything like what one might call due process, ordered his beheading. Had a small girl in a wheelchair not intervened and persuaded the Minister that deportation was preferable, this might have occurred. Other geologists were contracted to do the same job, found the same absence of an oil field, and fled the country on their own.

The story was soon reported to the press by one of the AWOL geologists, and other oil-rich nations had a good laugh—until they decided to check *their* oil reserves, and then their natural gas and coal reserves. Nation after nation was found to have carbon-based reserves of only around 20% of what had been there before. This led to a plunge in oil and gas stocks, auto stocks, and the stocks of other carbon-dependent companies. Meetings were held around the world to discuss how to adapt to this major decline in what many believed was the world's most important resource.

For decades, people had been talking about the need to reduce carbon emissions, to reduce the dependence on oil-producing nations, and to develop alternative fuels which were less destructive to the environment. But solar power, wind power, and hydroelectric power had been given slight attention while enormous profits were being raked in by a few well-positioned petrochemical entrepreneurs. Pollution, according to these lucky ones, was a problem solvable in the future. In the meantime, there was money to be made.

The President of the United States, himself an oilman, was livid when he heard about the shrinking of his own reserves in Texas. How could this happen? Was this just Mother Nature at work, or might it have something to do with the little girl? There was no direct link this time—not even a geographic one. But he was suspicious all the same. It was the kind of dirty trick this little creature might be capable of.

The second change manifested by the little girl related to climate. Throughout arid regions in the Third World—starting in the sands of the Sahara and moving across the Middle East all the way to Afghanistan and Western Pakistan, and even to Northern Mexico—rain began to fall as never before, not in torrents so as to cause flooding, but in periodic light storms. Deserts bloomed with green grass and flowers. Streams, ponds, and even lakes sprang up in places for the first time in centuries. The mostly poor inhabitants of these lands began to lose their fear of dying of thirst, and to enjoy the bounty of farming on fertile soil. Yes, there were some who found it hard to adapt to the new climate, but over time they, too, came to accept the new wealth.

Inside many of the new farmhouses, and alongside many of the lakes and streams, one could find crude statues, signs, crosses, crescents, and prayer wheels, all honoring the little girl.

The third change of this period was a direct relief of human suffering. For countless years, millions of people living in the earth's tropical zone had suffered and often died from malaria. The anopheles mosquito had killed more humans—particularly children, than any other predator. But suddenly, in one short moment in time, these mosquitoes and their terrible affliction were gone. No more malaria.

Pictures of the little girl appeared on the walls of hospitals in tropical zones, and parents of many faiths found time to mention the little girl in their prayers.

Scientists from around the world met to discuss these three simultaneous changes. Most agreed that the changes were good, and all agreed that they hadn't a clue as to how these things had happened so suddenly. There was mention of the little girl, but consideration of that possibility was generally dismissed as "unscientific."

There was a fourth change, which was not perceptible to scientists or others for several years.

Somehow, the little girl was able to tweak the fertility rates.

In affluent areas where the population was in serious decline—like Japan and much of Europe—they were raised. In poor, overpopulated areas—like Africa, South Asia, South America and the Middle East—they were tweaked downward.

The general effect of this was increased prosperity, although many husbands in the poor areas became furious at their wives' low child production and would have beaten them to death had it not been for the intervention of a few more Durgas and other such apparitions.

As Rich Barton read about these new changes on the planet, he remembered having had these visions. But he had no direct experience with drought, malaria, or infertility. Could it be that the little girl might respond to his mere thoughts?

"Daddy," said Peter, "is this little girl really only seven years old? She seems so smart for her age."

"Good question," he replied.

CHAPTER TWENTY

Trees Yielding Fruit

"I'm just a poor tomato farmer, raised in the fields of New Jersey," Lester Green used to tell people. "I used to think that life was as simple as planting, watering and harvesting the beautiful fruit and vegetables that God has given us."

Lester's early vision was shattered in the 1950s, when he went to rural India to study the relationship between food and population. "Yes," he told his friends, "the tomatoes still grow, but the population of the world is growing much faster. Sometime soon, there won't be enough to feed everyone."

Lester Green decided to dedicate his life to the concept of an environmentally sustainable economy. His soft blue eyes and unruly Einstein hair went with an easy smile, as he sought to persuade the leaders of industry and government to at least slow down the destruction of farmland and natural habitats. He worked for the U.S. Agricultural Department as an advisor on agricultural foreign policy for a time and, in 1974, founded the Worldwatch Institute. "This," he told people, "is nothing less than an attempt to save the world from our own reckless self-destruction."

The Institute became famous, and its annual publications on the State of the World, were widely read and respected. Lester wrote fifty additional books championing the need for humans to act responsibly toward their environment, and these were published in some forty languages. Lester received more than twenty honorary degrees and even more prestigious awards. Most people receiving such recognition would feel that their life had been a great success.

But underneath the accolades, Lester knew that he was failing in his mission. The health of the planet was deteriorating every year, every day, every minute, every second. He tried to accept the fact that it wasn't his fault. He was doing his best—was pouring every ounce of energy he had into turning things around. But the challenge was too great. Most humans were too ingrained in their patterns of consumption, and too focused on their daily lives, to be concerned with the larger picture. It wasn't that people were inherently bad or stupid. They were just short-sighted, and this was leading the human race to a point of no return.

On this day Lester was one of seven people sitting in a plush office of the largest timber mill on Papua, New Guinea. Outside, there was the incessant grinding of enormous saws cutting rare merbau hardwood into large logs, and the constant motors of huge trucks carrying these logs away to distant corners of the world. Inside the plush office, there were two Indonesian Government officials and two representatives of the Indonesian timber industry. Opposite them were three men: Lester and two other Americans trying to make a purchase.

"Look," Lester said to the Indonesians, "the bottom line is that we have enough money to make all of you and many more Indonesians rich. Ten billion dollars. That's unheard of in the annals of environmental programs. And if you want, there will be no strings attached—only that you fully protect your own wilderness areas and stop major logging in your country."

"Let us must remind you," added the President of the Nature Conservancy, "that your current annual harvest is more than sixty million cubic meters, and that at this rate you will not have any timber—zero, in ten years. This is a now-or-never proposition which your country cannot afford to refuse. Think of future generations. Think of your children and grandchildren. Think of our dear planet which gives us all life!"

"And I," said the foremost humanitarian musician in the world, "will sweeten the deal by offering whatever you might want in the way of art or music."

The four Indonesians, dressed in dark suits and shiny black shoes, walked to the back of the room beneath portraits of two of the bloodiest dictators of the twentieth century, Suharto and Sukarno. After several minutes of whispering, they came back to the Americans in a united front. One of them calmly said, "Twenty billion."

The faces of the three Americans dropped in visible disgust.

There was a long silence.

"Take it or leave it," said one of the Indonesians, coldly.

Without a direct answer, the three Americans started to walk out of the room. "This is far too much," Lester said softly to his friends. He was thinking, *I wouldn't trust these guys if it were a hundred billion dollars.*

At that point, a small girl in a wheelchair appeared in the room, with a woman and a man standing behind her. The seven men stared at the three strange figures. No one was scared, for she did not appear to pose a threat. But the girl looked directly at the four Indonesians for an awkwardly long time. They had heard rumors of such a creature, but never dreamed that she might someday appear before them in person.

Only one word was said before the three strangers disappeared as mysteriously as they had come. It was delivered in a local accent by the little girl, and it left an impression on everyone in the room.

It was the Indonesian word for "No."

Immediately afterward, the grinding sound of the large saws outside simply stopped. The loggers in the room made calls to their largest forest operations to check on how things were going. The answers they received were the same in tone and substance: "Disaster! All saws are down! Logging has stopped! No one is hurt, but no more trees can be cut until repairs are made!"

While the rest of the world was pondering the little girl's feat of tree preservation, Rich Barton had much bigger things on his mind. He was counting the few remaining stops after Indonesia on his last major trip, and worrying that after dealing with these items, the little girl would run out of things to do.

"Maria," he said, "I've got to get creative as never before. For some reason, I've been chosen to lead world reform, and I'm very unprepared."

"Honey," she replied, "don't you think it's time to reveal your special connection to this girl to everyone, and then work with world leaders on what to do next?"

Rich looked at her for a moment. Long black hair, dark sexy skin, perfect lips, cleavage that revealed small firm breasts. How was it that he, an achondroplasmian dwarf, had ended up with such a beautiful partner? It didn't make sense. And yet there were many things in this world that didn't sense.

He took her hand and led her gently into the bedroom.

Peter was asleep, and the world could wait.

CHAPTER TWENTY-ONE

The Waters in the Seas

"Dégoutant*,"* said the young marine biologist, as she climbed aboard the research vessel *Calypso V.* *"C'est vraiment dégoutant."* (Disgusting. It's really disgusting.)

Her name was Christiane Cousteau, a devoted granddaughter of the world's most famous oceanographer. As a child, her favorite memories were of sitting on his lap as he showed her movies he had made. "Look at this shark!" he had said to her. "He's a big one—and so gentle. Now watch, I am about to touch him."

He told her about his early days, when he invented the aqualung, later to be called scuba gear. "Before this," he told her, "people had only diving bells and big, heavy, metal suits tethered to the ship that restricted movement, and which few could afford." He told her about making *The Silent World*—a book, movie, and then TV show, which had opened the eyes of millions to the underwater wonders of the world.

While she was still a child, her famous grandfather moved his maritime focus from exploration to preservation. When she was old enough to join him on his "adventures," he would often point to oil slicks on the water, or to bottles and cans in the shallows below. "Christiane, my dear child," he would say, "look at what man has done to nature. It is really disgusting!" Christiane stood by him through the ups and down of his career. There were many awards, including ten Emmys for his television shows and the French Legion of Honor for his part in the French Resistance during World War II. There were also many conflicts—with environmentalists who accused him of abusing sea creatures to get good pictures, and with his own son Jean-Michel when they disagreed on the direction of the family's *Calypso Society.* She was there for him when his favorite son, Philippe, died in a seaplane crash in 1979, when his wife, Simone, died of cancer in 1990, and when he himself succumbed to a heart attack in 1997. In their last moments together in a Bordeaux hospital, her grandfather had given her his famous red knit hat, along with a whisper, "Please, my love, continue our work to save the seas."

The coastline of Indonesia, where Christiane was now diving, had recently been the scene of the worst *tsunami* the world had ever known. Over two hundred thousand people died in Indonesia alone. Hundreds of thousands were left homeless, and as many lost their jobs. The rich nations of the world had responded with massive relief for humans and their homes and infrastructure. But there was another area of damage for which relief had not been not so forthcoming: coral.

Christiane and other marine biologists were well aware that over 80% of the planet's large fish had disappeared in the last half of the twentieth century, along with more than half of the world's coral. Global warming, oil pollution and over-fishing were the major culprits, but Christiane felt that the biggest problem was what she called *"ennui"*—a disinterest on the part of almost all people and their leaders.

"They will give billions of dollars for a crisis that makes headlines, but have no interest in the steady collapse of basic ecosystems."

In this last dive, like most others before it, Christiane had discovered little evidence of damage from the *tsunami*, but a mountain of evidence relating to "garbage over time"—mattresses, boat parts, car batteries, broken air conditioners, huge torn fishing nets, styrofoam galore, tons of paper stuck together, and the ubiquitous containers of water, soda, and beer. Her water quality tests had revealed what was being found all over the world—an ocean ruined by crude oil, raw sewage and other man-made pollution. And she had also discovered the steady disappearance of coral—the prerequisite to life under water.

As the *Calypso V* motored back into the harbor, Christiane sat on the bow, legs draped over the side, watching the water and knowing that just about every square foot below was contaminated by human waste of one kind or another. *"Merde,"* she muttered as tears rolled down her face, "I wish my grandfather could be here to hold my hand."

On the shore, she saw a strange scene. Two figures stood on the beach—a man and woman, with a small girl in a wheelchair.

They were saying nothing, and a crowd had gathered. At this moment, the *Calypso V* was the only boat entering the harbor. It was as if the three figures on shore were awaiting its arrival.

When the *Calypso V* was still some fifty yards offshore, Christiane, for a very brief moment, caught the glance of the little girl in the wheelchair. Their eyes met, and Christiane immediately realized that the little girl was somehow reaching into her heart. Just a feeling. Some kind of touching of souls. What followed is highly controversial, because it made no sense whatsoever to most people who were not there. Nevertheless it shall be related in the same way as the newspapers reported it the next day from eyewitness accounts. The little girl and her companions moved toward the ocean. The sea water enveloped their feet, their legs, their torsos, their shoulders, and then their heads, until all three were totally submerged, wheelchair and all. At first, parts of them could be seen by the onlookers; and then, within a short time, they disappeared.

At first, no one knew what to make of this report. None of the three strangers had said anything. There was no clue as to what they might be doing in this muddy, polluted, *tsunami*-torn area.

But, within days, reports began to come in of large fish factory boats having equipment malfunctions. Most of them were forced to return to base for repairs. Other vessels using large nets to dredge ocean floors of all life were also forced to return home for repairs. Whaling vessels were rendered inoperable, as were large vessels of all kinds that were catching fish on a massive scale. Oil supertankers continued to move, but were unable to flush their tanks in the water as they had done before. This had to be done under the controlled conditions of drydock. On shore, there were strange reports of people being unable to dump garbage or sewage into the seas. It was like a protective shield had been placed around the oceans and seas, and mankind now had to think of other ways to get rid of its waste. Inside this protective shield, there was, incredibly, a massive cleansing of the ocean floor as vast amounts of mankind's garbage, oil, and sewage was removed. It took time, but the coral everywhere began growing back to its former condition of two hundred years earlier.

Rich Barton was busy working on his list. Overthrow the brutal dictator in Burma? Evict the Chinese from Tibet? No, he didn't have much time. He had to think bigger. Cure the world of global warming? Yes, that was better. But better still, how about altering human nature so that people weren't so selfish and cruel? Give them a new gene that would make everyone tolerant and loving.

But wait! he thought. *Don't we need both yin and yang, pleasure and pain, and good and evil in this world, to achieve balance and harmony? What would happen if there was no evil, no injustice, no freedom of choice? Would mankind then revert to a period of ignorance and blandness such as in the Garden of Eden?*

In contemplating these mighty questions, the tiny human mind of Richard Barton was overwhelmed.

CHAPTER TWENTY TWO

The Green Hell

T*he Amazon,* Rich Barton thought, as he sat at the desk in his study looking at an illuminated globe. *Yes, I'm so glad that's where she's going next. It's so massive, so important to mankind's survival, and so threatened—I've heard that up to 5% a year is being destroyed by marauders to make a fast buck. Yes that's it! Oh God, do we need her there! I can't wait!*

Of all the areas Rich had traveled to, he felt that he knew this one the best—not that anyone could begin to know the Amazon. Two million square miles of dense rainforest, much of it still unexplored, reaching into nine countries, with more water than the Nile and the Mississippi combined, pushing the Atlantic Ocean two hundred miles out to sea. Aside from humble ventures into small parts of it, no one could "know" the Amazon. But it was here that Rich had recently conducted his Ph.D. dissertation. He had vivid memories of the huge trees cut for logs floating down the river on barges. Each of these enormous trees had been a home for countless plants, animals, and even fish in the rainy season.

People were not starving in the Amazon. There was still enough fish and game to feed its small population, but its trees and animals were disappearing at an alarming rate, and the water itself was changing.

Yes, Rich thought, *I remember it like yesterday—the two Greenpeace people coming into Ari's café in Iquitos, joining me for a burger and then telling me that this city of three hundred thousand people had no sewage treatment plant!*

As in almost all towns in the Amazon Basin, the people of Iquitos were dumping their sewage directly into the nearest river. Granted, the Amazon Basin, rising and falling fifty feet a year across an area the size of a small continent, was a powerful force in its own right, and not easily subject to pollution. But, like the oceans, day after day of such abuse would change even its water quality, and would eventually make life for its animals, its fish, and even its humans, unsustainable.

Rich had seen *mineros* dredging the smaller rivers for gold, *petroleros* drilling for oil, *madureros* taking out large trees to barge downstream and sell abroad, and *casaderos* killing everything they could find, from jaguars to crocodiles, monkeys, snakes, and beautiful macaus and toucans.

So many of the tribes-people he interviewed had told him, "There used to be so many fish and animals around here that we could just go into the forest and find anything. Now we need to go far away just to find an armadillo or a wild pig for dinner."

Dunu was a proud member of the Mayoruna tribe. He was constantly moving back and forth across the Yavari River that separated Peru and Brazil, partly to attend to his four wives and their combined twenty-eight children, and partly to "keep an eye out invaders." He spent many days telling Rich Barton about his life—the endocannibalistic (family eating) practices of his tribe, the abduction of *mestiza* women for childbearing purposes, and the disappearance of fish and game in his area. Dunu was small—only 5' 4", and he had loved the company of an even smaller Rich.

"Reesh," he said in Mayoruna during their last meeting, "I wish all outsiders could be like you."

On this day, a band of Brazilian thugs came up the Yavari River in their speedy launch, looking for trouble. Around one of the river's many bends, they saw the most beautiful *kapoc* tree they had ever seen. They beached the boat, got out their chainsaws, and starting cutting.

When an older man waved his hands and said, "Stop, this tree is sacred," they shot him. When other villagers gathered and shouted at them, they laughed. And when Dunu shot one of them through the chest with an arrow, they brought out their guns and proceeded to kill every Indian in sight. They knew that there was no real law out here—most of the Amazon Basin was fair game for anyone with enough fire power. And they knew that if the Indians could be moved from this territory, the men could slash and burn this part of the jungle, mine it and farm it for a few years, make some money, and leave. They were young, strong and ruthless, and they dared anyone to stand in their way.

Dunu was high in a tree, looking down at two dogs and three invaders with guns, and saying his last prayer to a Pagan god, when they arrived—a man, a woman, and a little girl in a wheelchair who uttered one word in Portuguese to the men with the guns: "*Sai!*" (Leave!)

The invaders paid no attention to her and tried firing their guns at the man in the tree. Their guns backfired and their faces became bloody messes. They staggered back to their launch, told the others to forget the tree, and shouted to the Indians, "We'll be back!"

They never returned.

After this event, things changed in the Amazon Basin. Like Rwanda's *Parc National de Virunga*, like the Indonesian rainforest, and like the oceans of the world, the Amazon Basin became off limits to the destructive forces of mankind. When farmers, fishermen, hunters, loggers, and miners from the outside world came to destroy the forest or to take out large quantities of fish and game, they found the environment inhospitable. The region, which outsiders had long called "*El Inferno Verde*" (the Green Hell), came under the protection of a massive army of intolerable insects, poisonous snakes, diseases, *doendes* (spirits), and other strange forces.

What environmental conferences of the nine Amazon nations had been unable to achieve was achieved by the jungle itself, with help from a little girl and her two friends.

"I want her dead!" the President told his cabinet again, with blazing eyes, at their next meeting. "She's a threat to all we hold dear—our country, our values, and our *God!* Offer a reward of one—no, ten—billion dollars for information leading to her capture and death. We handled Al Qaeda. We handled Saddam Hussein. Surely we can handle this strange little creature and her sidekicks!

"And what's more," he added, forcefully, "let's raise the national security level to red, double the number of guards at our borders, triple the Coast Guard, and bring in the fleets and several Army and Marine divisions to guard both coasts! I have a feeling she's comin' our way!"

"Maria," Rich exclaimed while looking up at the moon on his back porch. "I think I know what we need most! More than anything, this planet needs a world government that's responsive to our real needs. I just don't know how to get there from here. How can we reform the United Nations Security Council, with all of its anachronisms and current tensions? How can we have a world democracy when most leaders don't trust each other? Again, I'm back to changing the basic nature of humankind, and I'm stuck on how to do this and whether or not this would be good!"

CHAPTER TWENTY THREE

The City of God

The border between America and Mexico had long been one of striking contrast. By daylight, America's large freshly painted houses in Chula Vista stood out against Tijuana's mud-colored huts and shacks with corrugated roofs. By night, American streetlights were much brighter than the dull glow of their Mexican counterparts. The long, high wire fence separating the two countries looked down on thousands of ragged wannabe Hispanic immigrants gathered in the hills on the south, and scores of mostly Caucasian border patrolmen in vehicles keeping guard on the north.

Carmen Rosario was only seventeen, and already the mother of two small children. Motherhood had not been her choice. Both times it had started in the middle of the night, when inebriated men she barely knew broke into her bedroom and took her amidst scratches and screams. She'd wanted to cross into America to seek her fortune; but now, with her two babies and with more determined American guards, she was too scared to try.

Money—to feed herself and her children, and to keep their tiny room—was essential for survival. She was prepared to do anything to get it, so she went to the Blue Fox nightclub in downtown Tijuana every night, hoping to find men willing to pay for her body, and hopefully not abuse it too much.

On this night, she thought she'd done well. The American was young, handsome, nicely dressed in brown slacks, and a little shy when they met. They agreed on a price, and went to a hotel room he said he'd just rented. But when they entered the room, there was a strange smile on his face. It was not the same look as when they met. Instead of making the normal advances, he just sat there on a wooden chair and watched her in silence. Then the door opened and a gang of six other young men burst in, with sadism in their eyes.

She tried to scream, but was soon gagged, stripped, and bound to the bed, helpless.

Oh my Lord, she prayed, while struggling for air through her nose, *all I want is to survive. Let them take my body. I don't need their money. I just need to be alive and well to care for my babies. Oh please, Lord, help me! Please, Lord, Santa Maria!*

And on that night, in the doorway of this room in the hotel, there suddenly appeared the form of a little girl in a wheelchair, with a man and a woman at her side. When the young men saw the intruders, one of them yelled "Get out of here!" and tried to push them out the door. When he was unsuccessful, his friends tried to slug the intruders, and one of them pulled a switchblade. At this point the little girl said, "No."

With that word, the seven sadists fell unconscious to the floor. The little girl wheeled her way to Carmen Rosario and took the gag out of her mouth. The ropes fell to the side of the bed, and the little girl looked deep into Carmen's eyes. Tears flowed as they hugged and Carmen said over and over, "Santa Maria . . . Santa Maria . . . Santa Maria!"

Later that night, when Carmen told people of "the miracle," Tijuana policemen went to the room, found the sadists still lying unconscious on the floor with their ropes still on the bed, and arrested them. The room and the hotel were turned into shrines, and Carmen became a kind of saint in the community, with no further financial cares.

Of more consequence was a large new development which mysteriously appeared on Mexican government land twenty miles east of Tijuana. Where there had once been stark brown rolling hills, there now stood a walled city with a large arch at its entrance.

Inside the walls were ten thousand brand new residences. Each new home was equipped with conveniences never before seen on Planet Earth. Every one had a kitchen with appliances for preparing meals, cleaning and laundry devices, a theater room with wall screens and multi-track sound systems, along with movies of people and places from far away in the galaxy. There were gardens filled with exotic new plants and trees, and nearby parks and schools with many advanced features.

To the right of the entrance was a theme park which was soon named "*El Futuro.*" It had fantastic rides into adventures, beauty and richness far exceeding anything yet produced at Disney World, Universal Studios or other such places in America. The advanced technology of this theme park was set to activate with complete safety at the mere push of buttons. Farther to the east were forests and farmlands with exotic new species of plants, animals, and insects awaiting the new residents and visitors.

Beyond that was a university and a medical school, both equipped with features from a society far more advanced than those found anywhere on Planet Earth. The governments of Tijuana and Mexico decided, in honor of this city's new celebrity, that Carmen Rosario herself should make decisions relating to who would live, work and visit there. After searching her soul, Carmen decided that in this border area in which the rich had so long exploited the poor, the glorious residences should be given only to local people who, like her, had been living on the bare edge of survival. Yes, there were objections by Tijuana's wealthiest citizens, who claimed that they should be able to buy these units "with proceeds going to the poor." Several American billionaires tried to buy anything they could with unheard of offers of money and bribes. But Carmen held fast to the spirit of "Santa Maria," and made sure that these fantasy homes went only to the poor.

There were many who believed that impoverished, mostly illiterate Mexicans could never manage and maintain such a complex enterprise, and that the new city would soon lapse into a state of corruption, crime, and chaos. But this didn't happen. As the new residents moved in, there was a spirit of community, integrity, hard work and peace which prevailed in what came to be known as the *Ciudad de Dios* (the City of God).

One other detail should be mentioned. Carmen insisted that the new city be open to all citizens of the world except for one group. She was adamant in her rule that "Not one single American citizen shall be permitted to enter the *Ciudad de Dios* until the American government opens its borders to the Mexican people."

Of course there were attempts by many Americans to breech the city's walls, or to sneak past attendants at the entrance. Some Americans hired "coyotes" for this purpose, but the city was impenetrable to its neighbors from the immediate north.

"Maria! Peter!" Rich yelled. "Get dressed in warm clothes! Bring your ponchos and sleeping bags! It might be cold! It might be rainy! And it could be dangerous! I don't care. It's time for all of us to go meet this little girl!"

"Is she smaller than me?" asked Peter.

"I don't know, Sweetie," Rich replied with a grin. "She may even be smaller than *me*!"

CHAPTER TWENTY FOUR

The Church

A s America braced itself for the arrival of the little girl and her entourage, several forces were in evidence. There was the American government, which had put the country on red alert and sent troops in camouflage fatigues and armored vehicles into airports, bus terminals, baseball stadiums, and other likely battle zones.

There was the media, which had its own red alert to try to find her first and somehow get her on the evening news, or maybe on Oprah or Barbara Walters. Their reasoning was that if she really wanted to change the world, then of course she would do it in the most effective way—through them.

There was a group of people who believed in what she stood for and relished the thought that she might challenge the President and make some needed changes. There was another group who believed her to be evil, and in the need to destroy her if the government didn't get her first. These groups held demonstrations and counter-demonstrations, with nasty epithets and threats of violence.

Then there were commercial opportunists who hung around any and all demonstrations, selling buttons, tee shirts, and dolls to anyone with a point of view.

What these groups had in common with all America and the world was an excitement—in some cases an apprehension—about where the little girl in the wheelchair might show up, and what she might do next.

Rich Barton drove his family to a small parking lot in the Tenderloin District of San Francisco. They walked to the entrance of the Glide Memorial Church on Ellis Street, a place where Rich and Maria had attended Sunday services many times. He knew the pastor, Rev. Cecil Robinson, a short black man with a golden voice, who had opened up the church to the homeless, the hungry, victims of violence, and people with AIDS.

Rich remembered Cecil telling him once, "Rich, why is it that I always feel like a giant when I'm around you?"

"It's my contribution to mankind," Rich had answered with

an easy smile.

Rich, Maria, and Peter walked two blocks down the street from Glide to a small park where large numbers of poor people had gathered. The night was cold and windy, and light rain had begun to fall. Maria turned to Rich and said, "Honey, is this another crazytime—like jumping out of the plane in the Congo rainforest?"

Rich smiled and said, "Maybe."

A long line of people had formed at a drinking fountain, but nobody was drinking the water. They were using it to clean their needles before injecting heroin, crack cocaine, and anything else that made them feel good.

"God damn!" one of them said, "Hurry up. I'm freezin' to death!"

"Well," Rich whispered to his family, "I guess we might as well settle in for the night." They placed their ponchos on the wet ground, put their sleeping bags on top, and rolled the other half of the ponchos over the top of the bags to keep them as dry as possible. They stuffed their outer clothes—hats, jackets, and sweaters—down to the bottom of the sleeping bags and then crawled inside them, with their bodies curled against each other to gather as much warmth as possible.

"Dad," said Peter, "Do you really think she's coming here?"

"I hope so," Rich replied.

At midnight, rain started coming down in torrents. Everyone in the park—Rich, Maria and Peter included—shivered in the wetness and cold. There were persistent sneezes and coughs, and Rich wondered whether some of his new neighbors would last the night.

By 3 am, the rain had slackened and most of the people were asleep. The human body can only stay awake for so long before succumbing to unconsciousness.

Shots rang out from two directions. After waiting a few seconds, Rich and Maria peered out of the openings at the top of their sleeping bags to try to see what was happening. The lamps in the park illuminated only a few trees and rainy blurs of figures on the ground. More shots, and then the unmistakable sound of an automatic weapon. There were shouts in English and Spanish, and then another automatic weapon opened up from different direction.

"What is this, Iraq?" someone yelled.

The sickening sound of gunfire continued for another two minutes—and then a slight figure appeared from the shadows.

"Hey Dad," Peter whispered. "Look!"

Rich was quiet for a while as his eyes tried to focus on a form that was making its way to the center of the park. Then, in a calm, considered tone, he replied, "There she is, son. Good grief, I was right!"

The rain stopped and there was silence as the little girl said in a soft voice that carried to all who were there, "Come."

She wheeled her chair toward the main entrance of the park, and for reasons which may never be known, the people who were shooting dropped their drugs and guns and followed her. Mostly in silence, she led them to the entrance of the Glide Memorial Church, where Rev. Robinson and his wife Nha were waiting.

"Welcome, brothers and sisters!" Rev. Robinson said as each wet and cold visitor walked through the open doors. "Welcome everyone! You have a home."

The night visitors were shown to warm showers, given clean clothes, and invited to sleep on mats on the floor of the sanctuary. But the people there had a sense that this night meant more than just coming out of the cold. As dawn broke through the stained-glass windows of the church, the Glide choir arrived and started singing *Oh Happy Day*. Many of the guests joined in and there was a feeling of coming together as never before.

But there was something else.

As the little girl in the wheelchair, attended by a man and a woman, watched the last of the wet, shivering humans enter the church from a spot near the organ, Rich Barton approached her and their eyes met. She looked directly at him and smiled.

It was that same powerful radiance which others had noticed

when she was just a baby.
It was also like a blast from a cannon.
Rich fainted.

As soon as reports came in that the little girl in the wheelchair had been spotted at Glide Memorial Church, American Marines raced over in their flack jackets, weapons drawn, hands on triggers, helicopters with spotlights overhead. They had instructions to kill her on sight—no talk, no negotiation, no surrender—just death to the enemy!

They found a group of mostly poor people who were basking in some kind of grateful glow. The soldiers were too well-trained to be deceived by this. If these people were too stupid not to recognize the enemy, that was their problem. The soldiers had a job to do. Of course they searched everyone, but no drugs or weapons were found. This lack of evidence infuriated some of the soldiers, who insisted that such articles must have been hidden somewhere in the church. Meanwhile the little girl and her two friends were nowhere to be seen.

Some of the American media reported the story with headlines like "America Invaded!" and "Enemy Turned Back at Church!" Reading these articles, one might think that the little girl had launched a military assault on Glide Memorial Church, and that the church had been saved only through the combat bravery of the Marines, with help from the Screaming Eagles of the 191st Airborne Cavalry. Other newspapers and broadcasters reported the more accurate comments of eyewitnesses.

Meanwhile, the continuing question was where the little girl in the wheelchair would go next. There was speculation about Denver, Chicago and Washington, D.C. The nationwide alert was raised from Red to Double Red, and the reward for information leading to little girl's capture or death was raised to include a full week in the White House's Lincoln Bedroom.

"This is serious!" the President proclaimed. "We're at war—and I'm so proud of our troops. This may be well our country's finest hour!"

When Rich Barton awoke from his fainting spell at the Glide Memorial Church, the little girl and her friends had gone. The first thing he said was, "Idiot! I'm an idiot! I finally get my chance to meet her, and what do I do? Faint! How could I be so stupid! So careless!"

"Honey," said Maria, "We should all count our blessings. This night, in many ways, has been the high point of our lives. Besides, we still don't know if the little girl can even talk."

Peter added, "Daddy, I *love* the little girl. I want to marry her!"

Such a thought had never crossed the generally imaginative mind of Rich Barton, and he had no immediate answer. Maria said, "Sweetie, don't you think you're a little young to be thinking of marriage now? Shouldn't you wait a few years?"

After briefly pondering the image of the little girl and her two friends sitting around the Thanksgiving table, Rich returned to the central question of his current life—what next? Glide Memorial Church was the last place he had visited on this last trip, and his last vision—about guns and drugs in America, would be coming soon. If the little girl's plan was to fulfill Rich Barton's visions from these last two trips, her mission on Planet Earth would soon be over! And the relationship between the man of ideas and the girl who implemented them would also be over.

During the next few days, almost all guns in America ceased to function. Handguns, rifles, and automatic weapons just stopped working, except for the police, the military, hunters, people at target practice, and those protecting their homes and work places. This, of course, produced an enormous outburst from everyone from street gangs and drug dealers to members of the National Rifle Association.

"Shooting is our right, as God-fearing Americans!" they exclaimed. "It's in our Constitution. We can shoot and kill anything we damn well please!"

The second change was more complex. It took a long time

for people to figure out what was happening. Two poppy-like flowers began to appear in the ground in cities and countrysides all over America. One was yellow, and people soon found that this was a marvelous stimulant. Eating one of these flowers made people feel happy without any side effects of aggression, anger or internal bodily harm. The other was blue, and people found this it to be a great relaxant. Eating one of these calmed people down, with no negative side effects or bodily harm. Eating more than one of these poppies in a 24-hour period made people sick, so no one did it more than once. Neither plant was addictive. People could go without their poppies for long periods without feeling symptoms of withdrawal.

Simultaneous with the introduction of the poppies came a reduction in the effects of commonly used (and abused) substances like alcohol, cocaine, heroin and tobacco. Hard as the users might try, no one could get more than a little high on any of these drugs. The poppies had more effect, and helped the addicts of the other drugs to transition to a much healthier life. Naturally, the vendors of addictive drugs were furious. But what could they do? Who could they blame? There was no choice but to accept the new, cleaner poppies.

Gangs and syndicates who had made a living off of this dark side of life had to adjust to a world without alcohol, illicit drugs, and guns.

A different country.

CHAPTER TWENTY FIVE

Speaking in Tongues

Once again the little girl in the wheelchair surprised people worldwide, when she turned up at the United Nations administration building in Geneva, Switzerland.

The Secretary General invited her into his office, told all attendants to leave, and closed the door. They stayed there for a full hour, as news bulletins flashed around the world and people wondered what could be going on. After all, she didn't really talk. She was only seven years old, and yet she was so strange that no one really knew what to expect.

At the end of the hour, the Secretary General opened his door to the glare of TV lights and flashes from still photographers, and announced that there would be a press conference in ten minutes.

The press room was overflowing with excited reporters as the small African man pressed his way through the crowd to a podium covered with microphones. For the first time in United Nations history, one of their press conferences was carried live on most broadcasting stations around the world.

The Secretary General read from a small paper: "Distinguished citizens of the world and friends of the United Nations, I have an announcement which should be of interest to all of you." He paused as journalists present and people watching worldwide on television leaned forward in anticipation.

"Two days from now, at 6 pm Eastern Standard Time in New York City, a special guest will speak to us, for the first and the last time, from the podium of the General Assembly."

He paused again.

"She has agreed to answer one question from every nation-member of the United Nations... It is my hope that everyone—*everyone* will accord her the courtesy and respect which is mandated in our United Nations Charter. Thank you."

Amid a flurry of flashing cameras and shouted questions, the small black man pushed his way back through the crowd and returned to his office, with strict instructions to his aides that he was not to be disturbed.

This press conference had different effects throughout the

world. In the Middle East, where the child had been born, there was pride and jubilation. Most people there saw her as a child of Islam, or at least of Abraham, and a force for peace and justice. In Africa, most people saw her as their hope for a better future. In most of Europe, Asia, and Latin America, she was already a hero.

New Yorkers had long believed that their city should be the center of the world, so they were particularly excited when they heard that the little girl in the wheelchair would make her first and only global appearance in their city. Many New Yorkers planned to gather outside the United Nations in the hope that they could catch a glimpse of this phenomenon.

Meanwhile, the U.S. President and his many American supporters were united as one in an effort to save the world from the destructive infidel. Whole divisions of armored vehicles were ordered to surround the area of the United Nations "to make sure she doesn't escape." Much of the U.S. Navy was positioned in nearby waters. Members of the National Rifle Association and private militias amassed at the United Nations Chapel, with their dysfunctional guns, to help the American military and "Fight for the Right to Fight." God-fearing Christians worked around the clock to produce buses and accommodations to make the journey to New York City, to protest against "the False Messiah," and to "Stand up for Jesus."

Some details of this event were obscure. Unlike other visitors to the United Nations, these guests needed no accommodations. The little girl and her two friends would not be staying at the Waldorf Astoria, the Plaza Hotel, or Trump Tower. Their living habits remained a mystery. Similarly, they needed no security guards. How they moved from one place to another without detection by the military and even the most diligent paparazzi was anyone's guess. And, according to the Secretary General, the little girl would need no translators. Somehow, she would communicate with everyone without assistance.

There was one other matter on people's minds. The Secretary General's statement included the words "for the last time." This implied that the little girl might be leaving in two days' time. Many on the planet had come to believe that she would solve all of the world's problems one by one, until none remained. If she left so soon, how could this be done?

Rich Barton was crestfallen.

CHAPTER TWENTY SIX

The Last Supper

For most of her time on Planet Earth, the little girl had lived amidst sorrow and social problems. On the last full day before her departure, she and her two friends apparently decided to experience some of the positive features of the planet, so they embarked upon what might be called a feast of the senses.

The weather on that day was mostly sunny planet-wide, with some squalls around the equator and two hurricanes arising in the South Atlantic Ocean.

The first report of a most unusual occurrence came from Geneva, where the immense fountain in the adjacent lake rose as usual, some one hundred feet in the air. Three bald eagles—two female and one male—were seen flying around it as if in jet formation, and then coming down low, riding the spout up, and being propelled up another hundred feet in the air. They did this three times each, and then, like schoolchildren playing on slides in a park, went off to another adventure.

Minutes later the three eagles were seen at Reichenbach Falls, where Sherlock Holmes and Professor Moriarty were reputed to have fallen to their deaths. Then they were seen by climbers at the top of Mont Blanc, the Eiger and the Matterhorn. Tourists on the Eiffel Tower saw them perched together at the very top, and then passengers of a *Bateau Mouche* boat saw them land on a railing just feet away.

A short time later they were seen at Versailles, then at Britain's gigantic Ferris wheel, and then playing for a time with ravens at the Tower of London. They were said to have had a gleeful energy, full of play and devoid of aggression.

The three eagles reportedly turned back to France's island city of Saint Michel, where the tide was in, and then on to the Pyrenees, the Rock of Gibraltar, and Rome, where they played for a while in a large fountain. They flew past the window of the new Pope, who waved. And then on to Jerusalem, where Christians, Muslims, and Jews also waved. Then they went south, and were seen circling the *Kaaba* at Mecca seven times. They were seen above a wildebeest herd in the Serengeti Plain, and at the top of Kilimanjaro. Then at Victoria Falls, the Zimbabwe ruins, and riding immense wind currents over South Africa's Table Mountain. They were seen at India's *Taj Mahal* in Agra, at the ornate temple at Madurai, and eating perfumed dust out of the hand of Sai Baba in Bangalore.

When they arrived at the Dalai Lama's home in Dharamsala, he had already set out food and water for them. They lingered there, as if in conversation, and then flew on over the Himalayas.

The Charles Bridge in Prague, Russia's Winter Palace at Petrograd, the Great Wall of China, the Cambodian ruins of *Angkor Wat,* and *Ayers Rock* in Australia—these were just a few of the many sightings of the three eagles on that day.

Another part of this story may seem less credible, but it, too, was reported by a number of eyewitnesses. Three dolphins were seen swimming, jumping, and then seemingly flying over the Pacific Ocean as they cavorted with the large fish around them. There was one report of more than a hundred whales playing with them, and another of thousands of dolphins and tuna swimming in a single school.

In South America three eagles were seen over Macchu Picchu in Peru, Iguazu Falls in Argentina, and Angel Falls in Venezuela. In North America they were seen watching the divers at Acapulco, flying low over Tijuana's new *Ciudad de Dios,* and above the glorious lodge at Banff, Canada. At San Francisco's Pac Bell Park, they landed on the right field wall just as Barry Bonds came to bat. After watching him take two balls, they saw Bonds deliver the third pitch over the wall within feet of where they were perched, and the ball splashed in the waters of McCovey Cove.

Other American sightings of three bald eagles were reported on Mount Shasta, Disneyland, the Grand Canyon, Chicago, Crawford, New Orleans, Monticello, Boston, and Washington, D.C. The last sightings were at New York City's Statue of Liberty, and at the site where the World Trade Center had once stood.

CHAPTER TWENTY SEVEN

Epiphany

Music was in the air on the day of the little girl's final appearance on Planet Earth. New Yorkers, proud of again being the center of attention, blasted their favorite song on speakers in streets and stores, with a slight twist:

> *Start spreading the news, She's comin' today.*
> *I want to—be a part of it, New York, New York ...*

In London they were singing George Harrison's song:

> *Something in the way she looks,*
> *She loves us like no other lover.*
> *Something in her style that shows me.*
> *I don't want her to leave us now,*
> *Don't want her to leave us now. . .*

In Rwanda, Tanzania and other Swahili speaking nations, they were singing:

> *Malaika, ninakupenda malaika . . .*
> *(Angel, I love my angel . . .)*

There were other songs of love for an angel being played and sung in Brazil, China, India, Indonesia, Egypt, Iran, Iraq, Israel, and Palestine. A thousand gospel choirs were singing Amazing Grace in different languages from South Africa to Senegal, and in many churches across England and America. In the United States there were also many angry groups forming to protest the activities of the little girl.

By 4 pm Eastern Standard Time, most of the people on the planet had gathered in homes, schools, theaters, squares, churches, mosques, and synagogues to witness what would later be called the greatest television event in history.

Rich Barton was unusually quiet that day, as he sat with Maria and Peter before the television in their living room. He was feeling both guilty and apprehensive.

Rev. Cecil Robinson was also quiet as he sat with an overflow crowd before a large screen at the Glide Memorial Church.

David Plotkin had gathered his magician friends to witness

the event in his Taj Mahal.

The Dalai Lama was watching a television from the same living room in Dharamsala, where he had met with Rich Barton years ago.

A large screen had been erected in Beijing's Tiananmen Square, where millions had gathered, another in Red Square in Moscow, and others in London, Paris, Rio, Rome, Tokyo and cities throughout the world.

The U.S. President was in the only place he considered appropriate for such an occasion—the War Room, deep beneath the White House, with most of his cabinet and the Joint Chiefs at his side.

"I don't care what anybody else is calling it," he declared. "To me, it's a war, and I aim to be on the winning side."

He had given strict orders for his troops to be on "instant alert to start firing—and not to care about casualties. Don't hold back! We may lose a few thousand, hell, a few million—but we're not going to lose this war!"

In support of the President, an enormous crowd had gathered outside the United Nations General Assembly building to protest the guest speaker and what she stood for. Many were carrying signs with messages like, "We Don't Want You!" and "Just Go Home!"

Television cameras dutifully covered this huge protest rally and others like it in cities across the United States. Most people in other parts of the world, who truly loved this little girl, couldn't understand the anger of these Americans. They were shocked.

There were also rallies in support of the little girl at the United Nations headquarters. These included peace groups, religious groups, and others, but these groups were mostly calm and quiet. Some of them lit candles as the sun slipped over the horizon. Some were deep in prayer.

The General Assembly meeting room is equipped to handle delegates from more than two hundred nations, as well as aides and special guests. Earphones for more than a hundred languages are available for major speeches, but on orders of the Secretary General, no interpreters were present on this occasion.

Between 4 pm and 6 pm there was TV filler programming, mainly interviews with people who had met the little girl. Several survivors of the Janjaweed incident were interviewed in their new, safe village. Mary Njathi told people about how the little girl had cured her village of AIDS, and other AIDS survivors from across the globe told their stories. There were interviews with Russians who had witnessed the little girl's atomic bomb intervention, with patients in Beijing and Bangkok who had recovered from pulmonary disorders, and with the New Delhi bride who barely escaped being burned to death. The last was with Carmen Rosario, who was quite moving in her praise of the "Santa Maria."

As the U.S. President watched all this, he began to feel uneasy. He sensed that something was wrong, but couldn't quite put his finger on it.

At 6 pm Eastern Standard Time, the Secretary General walked into the General Assembly auditorium and up to the podium. Most of the other delegates stood and clapped. Some of them cheered. As the delegates and others sat down, the room became quiet, except for the unmistakable shouts of "U-S-A! U-S-A!" from angry protesters outside.

The Secretary General looked around for a moment, making eye contact with everyone in the room, and said, "Delegates, friends, and citizens throughout our beautiful world, we have here this evening an extraordinary guest who has, in her own way, tried to serve the people on this planet. To be honest, I do not know much about her. I don't even know her name. But I do know that she is a wonderful person, and that she deserves our respect, our friendship, and our courtesy, particularly on this special occasion."

He paused.

"She has agreed, at my request, to answer one question from each of our member nations. So without further commentary, here is our guest."

The Secretary General walked to his seat near the podium and sat down. The podium was empty. There was no movement from any of the doors, or from any of the people inside. The room was silent. All that could be heard were the chants outside of "U-S-A! U-S-A!"

Much of the world was apprehensive.

Suddenly, as if by magic, a little girl in a wheelchair appeared in front of the podium, and a man and woman appeared behind her. All three were dressed in simple robes. They were solemn, as the only sound that could be heard was the chant of "U-S-A!" from outside.

As the three manifested their bodies at the United Nations, a great cheer went up in David Plotkin's Taj Mahal. *"Yes!"* the magicians shouted. *"Do it again!"*

One of them said. "I could do that!"

Another exclaimed, "I could too—just give me ten minutes head start!" They all laughed.

In the General Assembly, there was an awkward silence. Then, unexpectedly, the U.N. Ambassador from China stood up, clapped his hands, and emitted a loud cheer which burst forth in a distinctively un-Chinese fashion. This was followed by many other delegates standing, clapping, cheering, and making other wild noises of praise for what she had done for their countries.

The American Ambassador, as instructed, did not leave his seat or make a sound. Some of the TV cameras captured a scowl on his face.

"Shall we move in now, sir?" asked the Secretary of Defense, deep in the White House bunker.

"No, not yet," the President replied.

The wild applause and cheering went on for a full fifteen minutes—unheard of in the history of this room. At one point, the little girl in the wheelchair changed her expression from solemnity to a smile, and this brought to the whole room—and much of the watching world, an explosion of laughter and joy.

The Secretary General used his gavel to quiet the room, and then asked the little girl if she wanted to make an opening statement. She shook her head to say no. People were reminded that this was a creature who had not yet, in seven years of life, ever uttered more than one word at a time. There was still no evidence that she knew how to talk.

"In that case," said the Secretary General, "we will move to one question from each delegation. The first is Afghanistan."

Afghanistan's new United Nations Ambassador stood up in his colorful tribal robe and asked, "Who are you?"

The little girl paused for five seconds. Then she answered in all the languages of people listening throughout the world, in the tone of a small girl with excellent elocution:

"I am a life form from an area you have not yet discovered. My name, my true form, and the location of my home are beyond your capacity to understand. But in other ways, I am a being seeking fulfillment, just like each of you."

The noise of the protesters outside grew louder. "U-S-A!" morphed into "Je-sus Saves!" The intense anger on the protesters' faces made it feel more like "Je-sus Hates!"

The U.S. President, already uncomfortable from listening to the earlier parts of the broadcast, and from seeing such support for the little girl from nations around the world, grew restless.

The next question came from Albania. "Are you the Messiah?"

"I am what I am," came the reply. This direct quote from the *Bible* shocked the Christians, who didn't know quite what to make of it. The little girl went on to explain. "To me, I am a being seeking fulfillment, like each of you. And to each of you, I may be something different—whatever you may find in your soul."

Furious and out of control, the protesters pushed their way through the first of three barriers between them and the General Assembly building. The lines of New York police were no match for the thousands moving forward with one objective: destroy the infidel.

The U.S. President assumed his "deer in the headlights" look. There was some voice coming from deep inside that was warning him. He mumbled, "This is turning into a God-Damned lynch mob."

"Sir," said the National Security Advisor, "that's your base."

"I know," said the President. "They actually mean well."

"Ready to attack the girl?" asked the Secretary of Defense.

"No," said the President. "Not yet."

The next question came from the representative from Angola: "Why did you come here?"

"I came to your planet, which you call Earth, in order to help your species avoid extinction. My projections indicate that a combination of advanced weaponry, neglect of the poor, and wanton resource destruction is likely to bring about your demise within the next one hundred years. My few interventions have been indicators of how you might avoid such destruction."

The protesters reached the second barrier. It was a sea of angry humanity, which no police force on earth could have contained. Nearby, the supporters of the little girl knelt in silence, held their candles, and prayed openly to their gods or higher powers.

"Is there any way our boys, our good American troops, can stop this crowd?" the President asked.

"Sir," replied the Secretary of Defense, "with all due respect, our mission all along has been to keep the enemy from escaping, not to protect her."

"So what could we do now to protect her and the others in that building?" asked the President.

"Not a whole lot," the Secretary replied. "The crowd's too close. We could, of course, drop a bomb—a smart bomb, on the whole area, but that would also destroy those in the building. Uh, Mr. President, sir, remember what you said about casualties?"

*****

The delegate from Argentina asked, "Why do you care about us?"

"I have watched your planet for a long time, and I see many beautiful parts of your culture. But the real answer is much more simple. Why does a mother care for her child? Why do friends become close? In my world, compassion is all-important, and I feel love toward each of you and your species."

At that moment, there occurred, in some ways, the greatest miracle of all.

It was a transformation of only one man, but such a key man that historians later wrote about this as a turning point in the history of the planet.

The U.S. President was watching television coverage in the War Room, with his generals and other staff, when somehow, in an instant of time, he saw the little girl as an angel.

Was it like Paul on the road to Damascus, Moses on Mount Sinai, or Mohammed in the cave near Mecca?

Who knows?

Such events are difficult to comprehend.

In this instant the U.S. President ceased to see the little figure in the wheelchair as a threat to Christianity, and instead, as a part of it. And America was seen not as a military power ordained by God to save the world through force, but as a nation with a humble responsibility to avoid war and to help other nations and people in need.

On the television screen in front of him, the hate in the eyes of the mob became the hate of those who had crucified Jesus, and the President saw himself in the unique role of Pontius Pilate.

Such transformation of a belief system does not come easily. To have one's lifetime friends become adversaries, and one's lifetime adversaries to become friends, requires major processing over time. But the President did not have the luxury of time. He needed to act now, to reverse course as best as possible in whatever way he could.

As he watched the protesters break through the second

barrier, the President got to his feet. "Take me there!" he said decisively to an aide. "I want the fastest helicopter we've got! Go on, *move, move! Let's go!*"

"Yes, sir."

The Armenian delegate asked the little girl, "If you truly care for us, then why don't you help us more—like curing cancer and diabetes, and bringing riches to all in the Third World?"

The little girl paused before answering. "Ultimately, this question is about immortality. If each of you lives indefinitely, and if you also continue to have children, then your planet will not be able to sustain your species and you will become extinct even faster. I'm not prepared to do this."

The protesters had been temporarily stopped by the second barrier. It was a series of metal gates chained together, which could not be pushed aside. The frenzy persisted, and a new slogan was shouted by all:

"Aliens and atheists, leave us alone! We don't want you—go back home!"

The President watched the scene from a television in his helicopter, his eyes glued to the screen. The broadcast cut to enormous crowds in Manila, and then Delhi and Sao Paulo, all praying in silence for peace on the planet, then back to the shouting United Nations protesters.

"ALIENS AND ATHEISTS, LEAVE US ALONE!
WE DON'T WANT YOU! GO BACK HOME!"

Some were waving their fists and throwing rocks.

"Thank God they don't have guns," the President mumbled.

"Sir?" asked his aide, who had not been able to make out his leader's words.

"Nothing," replied the President.

"What can you tell us about the universe?" asked the

Australian delegate.

"Perhaps I can answer your question best by distinguishing between your universe and mine. As I understand it, your universe includes galaxy clusters extending to around thirteen billion light years from your planet, and reaching inward into the quantum mechanics level of quarks. What you call 'the universe' is only one of more than a hundred universes of which I am aware. The universe in which I was born is many levels in time, space, and other dimensions beyond what you call 'the universe.'"

"Mr. President, an aide exclaimed, "the crowd's climbed over the second barrier. They're almost at the building."

The President was deep in thought, trying to figure out what to do. "Can't this thing go any faster?" he yelled to the pilot.

"What's your religion?" asked the Austrian delegate.

"Please let me answer this question in three parts." (The President was thinking that with this crowd she would never get to Part Two.) "First, we have no cosmology. Even with our advances, we have no understanding as to how existence came to be. Second, we are spiritual, and compassion is at the core of our belief system. Third, we have no evidence of a higher power intervening in our lives. We believe that we are all on our own to sustain and improve life."

The protesters were now facing a combination of New York policemen and United Nations troops at the third and last barrier. Ordinarily a crowd would be wary of moving further, but this group was fighting for God and country. Death was a small price to pay.

Bullhorns told them that they would be shot if they went further, but many of them didn't care. Protesters began the charge. Shots rang out.

"Oh no!" the President yelled. "We're too late!"

*****

The next question came from Azerbaijan (which had been promised one billion dollars in U.S. military aid if it was asked). "What do you think of America's leadership in bringing freedom and democracy to the world?"

Once again the girl paused before answering. "I believe that there are two kinds of freedom," she said. "The first is freedom from suffering—from things like hunger, disease, poverty and despair. For these kinds of freedoms, America has done little compared to what it could do." She paused, as the shouting grew louder.

"The other kind of freedom is political and behavioral. For many years, the American government has placed its own self-interest above freedom for other peoples, and the current President has yet to learn that real freedom cannot be achieved at gunpoint."

The shouting grew louder still.

"As for democracy, your planet is far behind. Real democracy means all people having the right to participate in important decisions. Your planet has more than seven billion people, but only a few of the six percent who live in America have an effective voice in major decisions. This is not democracy."

At this point the mob, with some having fallen and been trampled, broke for the General Assembly building. One of the first to arrive threw a smoke bomb into the main chamber. As the black, sooty smoke disrupted the quiet scene, most of the delegates knelt to pray.

They had nowhere to go.

They had assumed that, with the most powerful military in the world, America would protect them from harm. Now they realized that perhaps they were part of a giant trap to murder the little girl. The President, all along, had planned to use this room as a death chamber for her, her two friends, and everyone else who happened to be there.

It was hard to believe this theory, but nothing else made sense.

They looked at the guest speaker—small, frail, so mysterious. The little girl in the wheelchair was crying, as she had so many other times in the past few months. And as the television cameras focused on that tiny face, most of the world cried with her.

What happened next was, as on other occasions, difficult to understand. Cameras recorded it, but people still aren't sure what really happened. At the moment the mob arrived at the doors of the General Assembly room, an invisible shield enveloped the room to protect all who were inside. The mob proceeded to beat their fists against the shield and scream,

"DEATH TO SATAN! DEATH TO THE GIRL!!
DEATH TO THE ALIEN WHO'S COME TO OUR WORLD!!"

The roof of the General Assembly building was not flat and certainly not made for helicopter landings. When the President told his pilot to land there, he was told, "Mr. President, that would be very dangerous."

"I don't care!" the President shot back. "That roof is the only place with no people on it, and I need to be there. Do it! That's a direct order from your Commander-in-Chief!"

The helicopter made a wobbly landing on a sloped area of the roof, and tilted far to the right side, almost bringing the overhead rotor blade in contact with the roof, which would have resulted in a crash and explosion. But the pilot, the President, and his aide survived the landing. The President ran to the roof's edge, saw the mob beating their fists against the shield, and yelled through a bullhorn, "Go home! Y'all go home! Everything is under control!"

At first the mob couldn't believe that this was their President—in rolled-up shirt-sleeves, no less. But the voice was unmistakable—and so were his face and body. They looked up at him, pointed to him, and got the attention of the others. It took a full fifteen minutes, but the President turned the mood around and persuaded them to stop what they were trying to do and go home.

Then the President jumped down to the walkway and made his way to the front door. As witnesses later reported, the shield opened and the President walked into the General Assembly room. People from nations around the world were there, praying for safety for themselves and peace for their planet. The air was still black from the smoke bomb, and had a sick burning smell. The President made his way directly to the podium area, where he saw, in person for the first time, the little girl in the wheelchair. She was a tiny figure, much smaller than he had imagined. She was just sitting there, crying quietly to herself.

The President walked over to her, tears in his eyes, put his arms around her, his head on her shoulder, and said, "I'm sorry. I'm so sorry! Please forgive me."

The two stayed in that posture, motionless, for a long time. Television cameras broadcast the scene in close-up, with no commentary, to millions—billions, around the world.

There was no need for narrative. Words had no place.

At last, with most of the world weeping with them, the little girl raised her head and looked directly into the eyes of the President. It was the face of an angel, the face of suffering, the face of innocent children looking for a future.

The President whispered something in her ear. She smiled and looked at him. When she whispered something back, the President's face broke out with a smile as big as all Texas.

After one more long embrace with the President, the child looked out at the General Assembly and all the cameras. In a soft, sad voice, she said: "It's time to go now. Farewell, Richard Barton. Farewell, President Bush. Farewell, my friends. I love you all."

And she and her two friends disappeared.

TWENTY EIGHT

Resurrection

A t the time, it was widely assumed that the little girl in the wheelchair and her two friends had left the planet, never to return. They had accomplished their stated mission—of giving "indicators" of how humankind might survive. They had experienced some of the richness—both joys and sorrows—of the human condition, and they had shared love with many of its people.

But there was one more surprise to come.

That same night, several hours later, the little girl and her friends suddenly appeared simultaneously in millions of homes, synagogues, temples, churches, mosques, town squares, schools, hospitals, orphanages, and many other places, all over the world. How such a tiny frail thing and her two friends could suddenly multiply into so many identical forms no one knew, or could even guess. But then, as has been said, there are many things about these three visitors that will never be understood.

Somehow, the threesome knew which homes and people not to go to. There was no reason to intrude where they were not wanted.

One of the places where they lingered was David Plotkin's Taj Mahal. After appearing there suspended in air to great cheers and applause, they invited the magicians to join them on a "cruise" around Las Vegas. And that night, no less than twenty-five magicians were seen flying through the air, doing cartwheels and loop-de-loops and all sorts of maneuvers.

The three figures also lingered with the people they knew best: Mary Njathi, Rev. Cecil Robinson, Carmen Rosario, Dunu, the bride from India whom they had saved, the people they had met at the pulmonary wards in Bangkok and Beijing, and so on.

In Rich Barton's living room, the little girl and her two friends hugged Rich, Maria, and Peter for a long time. When at last Rich pulled away, he looked at her, tears in his eyes, and asked softly, "What should I do now?"

This time, again, as was her custom, she offered only one word in reply: "Serve."

Several months after the departure of the little girl and her friends, Barbara Walters interviewed the two primary figures in this story.

The first was Richard Barton, who was seen in his plush office at the Ashland headquarters of his new Earth Institute. "Barbara," he said, "the purpose of this organization—and of my life—is to heed the warnings of the little girl, and to reverse the present destructive trends on our planet."

"Tell me, Richard," said Ms. Walters. "Honestly now, do you believe that this little girl will somehow come back to make your new dreams for our planet come true?"

"I have no idea," he answered. "I only know that fate has given me a mission to try to make this a better world."

Later, Barbara Walters was invited into the Oval Office for an interview with the President. For the first few minutes, pleasantries were exchanged. Then Barbara put on her "serious face," and asked the question that was on everybody's mind. "Mr. President," she said, "could you tell us what, exactly, you whispered into the ear of the little girl at the General Assembly room, and what, exactly, was her reply?"

The President shrugged. "Barbara," he said, "I guess you folks might as well hear it now as anytime.

I asked her, 'Are y'all comin' back?' And after givin' me a smile, she whispered in my ear, 'maybe.'"

###

Acknowledgments

In October of 1998, as a social worker for Sierra Adoption Services, I visited a foster home in Sacramento. There were three young children living there, and one of them was an African American girl by the name of Elicia. She was five years old, and she was in a wheelchair because her legs were withered. Every time I visited that home, Elicia greeted me with the biggest smile I had ever seen. And each time I thought to myself, *If this little girl, with this great handicap, can exude such joy, then who am I to ever complain about anything at all?* She is the model for the heroine in this story.

There are several chapters in this novel which drew upon personal experiences. During my year in Israel's Kibbutz Galed (1971), I worked in the orchards with Michael and Yitrak and they told me about their lives escaping Nazi Germany. During my trip to Africa in 1976-77, I lived with the Kikuyu family of Mary Njathi, camped with Asumbo's Pygmy community in Zaire, and met some of Dian Fossey's gorillas. During my year in India and Nepal (1981-82), Lakpa was my Sherpa guide for thirty days as we trekked to the base camp of Mt. Everest. and later I later interviewed the 14th Dalai Lama of Tibet in his Dharamsala living room. During my dissertation field work in the Peruvian Amazon (1995, I lived in the thatched hut of Mayoruna tribesman Dunu while he told me his life story.

I've been to Tijuana several times, and each time I was disturbed by the disparity between rich Americans and poor Mexicans living just across the border. And I've attended many services at San Francisco's Glide Memorial Church, and marveled at the way in which Rev. Cecil Williams celebrated life with people of different races, cultures and socio-economic backgrounds.

In the chapter on United Nations history, I used information presented in Stanley Messler's *United Nations: The First Fifty*

Years. For the chapter on Mecca, I used details recalled for me by my mental health colleague, Mo Tayeb. And in the chapter on AIDS, I felt the presence of my good friend Dan Turner, who worked with me on his autobiography before dying from this disease in San Francisco in 1989.

For the chapter on magic, I'm indebted to "The Amazing" Marc Mesmer for letting me be his apprentice. David Copperfield gave me deeper amazement in several of his shows, and I enjoyed talking with him after one of them. Some of the detail in this chapter on magic was taken from a program of Copperfield's 2004 World Tour, and some was taken from Milbourne Christopher's *Magic: A Picture History.* My fondness for magic extends back over twenty-five years, during which I have given over 300 small shows. Next year I'll be rewarded by induction into the International Brotherhood of Magicians' Order of Merlin.

I had some fun with the caricature of our current president and his administration. However, behind the humor, I believe that one of the world's biggest problems is the attitude of superiority of many people in the United States. The sudden conversion of President George W. Bush at the end of the book is meant as a ray of hope—that mainstream America and its leaders may someday come to respect our neighbors and treat them as worthy members of the human family.

Some of the characters in this novel clearly represented real people in the world today, even though the full names were seldom used. These included Kofi Annan, Lester Brown, George W. Bush, David Copperfield, the Cousteau family, Dian Fossey, the 14th Dalai Lama of Tibet, Barbara Walters and Oprah Winfrey. I believe the general points of view of these people were consistent with the presentations of the book, and an apology is offered here if there was any problem in this regard.

Jane Roach has been my close friend and partner in developing Sierra Dreams Press and its website. The primary editor has been Walter Kleine—a man with charm, vision and a sense of detail. The cover and chapter artist has been Phawnda Moore, who met the challenge of producing images to correspond to the story and its mystery. Jeff Hendriksen took the photograph on the back cover from a spot near my home.

It should also be mentioned here that the warmth and gentleness of the little girl comes from my father, Stuart Jr., and the book's spirit of joyful defiance comes from my mother, Kay.

Finally I wish to acknowledge the extended Rawlings and da Silva families for their support through the years, and to my wife Elsa and son Austin for their constant love.

As I ponder the next hundred years of our civilization, I'm worried about most of the trends. But I'm also very grateful to have richness in my everyday life, and to be sharing it with people like you.

Stuart

Sierra Dreams Press

Sierra Dreams Press was founded by Stuart Rawlings and Jane Roach in 2005, with the purpose of publishing some of Stuart's written and musical works, and the works of others as well. Its website now offers these items:

The God Child Trilogy

Another Messiah (novel written in 2005)

Delusions (sequel written in 2012)

The God Child (sequel written in 2019)

*Now available in paperback, e-book
and audiobook formats*

Other Books

My Favorite Quotations, Volumes 1-8 (1971, 1976, 1981, 1986, 1991, 1998, 2007 and 2018)

Good Soldier Wolf (by Jiri Wolf and SR, 1992)

IVS Experiences: from Algeria to Viet Nam (Edited by SR, 1992)

Auburn's Creative People (2), by SR and Jane Roach (2007 and 2008)

Love Interrupted, Lila Guerrero (Autobiography, 2000)

The Monster in the Cave, (children's book by Austin and Stuart Rawlings, 2009)

CDs

Memories (CD of 26 songs performed by SR)

Life is a Treasure (CD of 20 songs written and performed by SR)

Christmas in Auburn (CD of 20 songs performed by SR and the Auburnaires, 2008)

Auburn, U.S.A. (CD of 20 songs performed by SR and the Auburnaires, 2005)

Videos

(look in YouTube under Stuart Rawlings)

I Like Junk Food, by SR and David Anastasiou, 2011

Austin's Dream, by SR and David Anastasiou, 2010

Lucky Man, by SR and the Auburnaires, 2010

All the books and CDs are available through:
Sierra Dreams Press
15200 Wild Oak Lane
Auburn, CA 95603
(530) 878-8831
www.sierradreamspress.com
stuartrawlings@hughes.net

"Life is precious, and there is no time to lose."